SIDEWALK INDIAN

Books by Mel Ellis

FLIGHT OF THE WHITE WOLF
IRONHEAD
SAD SONG OF THE COYOTE
WILD GOOSE, BROTHER GOOSE
SOFTLY ROARS THE LION
RUN, RAINEY, RUN
THIS MYSTERIOUS RIVER
CARIBOU CROSSING
THE WILD RUNNERS
PEG LEG PETE
NO MAN FOR MURDER

Mel Ellis

SIDEWALK INDIAN

Holt, Rinehart and Winston
New York Chicago San Francisco

Library of Congress Cataloging in Publication Data

Ellis, Melvin Richard
Sidewalk Indian.

I. Title.
PZ4.E4663Si [PS3555.L615] 813′.5′4 73-13980
ISBN 0-03-012076-4

Printed in the United States of America: 065
Designer: Robert Reed
First Edition

SIDEWALK INDIAN

Charley Nightwind closed the door softly. He stood for a moment as though bewildered. Then he turned the key, and the lock snapped shut. Picking up a cardboard suitcase, and walking quietly, he came slowly down the worn stairs, knocked at the landlady's door, and when she appeared handed her the key.

"Where will you go?" the landlady asked.

The boy shrugged.

"You may stay here you know." The landlady's eyes were bright, as if with tears.

"Thanks, but no. I don't need an entire apartment, only a room."

"Do you have a job?"

"I'll get one," Charley told her.

"Well, if you can't find one just remember you are always welcome here."

The boy thanked her again, and turning went down the hall with its flaking paint, looked once at the empty mailbox on the wall, stepped out, and was at once engulfed by the sights, sounds and smells of the big city.

At the White Tower restaurant on the corner he ordered a hamburger for breakfast. "Coffee? Milk?" the waitress asked. Charley shook his head and washed down a bite of hamburger with water.

The restaurant door opened to let in a bearded youth. "Well, if it isn't the Sidewalk Indian," the youth said, putting a hand on Charley's shoulder.

Charley looked down at the hand on his shoulder but made no move to shrug it off. The young man, seeing the look, lifted his hand and let it fall to his side.

"I'm sorry, Charley," the bearded boy said. "I'm sorry," he repeated, "sorry to hear about the death of your mother."

Charley shrugged, an almost imperceptible gesture.

"How'd it happen?" the youth asked.

Charley turned, looked at the young man almost as if to see whether he really wanted to know, or if he was merely making conversation, and then said quietly, "Heart."

The young man opened his mouth as though to speak again, closed it, and then abruptly went back out the door.

Charley tried to finish his sandwich, but couldn't. It was dry as sawdust in his mouth. He put the hamburger down, took a sip of water, and then getting up started toward the door.

"Hey, you forgot to pay," the waitress called after him.

Blood rushed to the boy's face. "I'm sorry," he said, turning.

"Yeah, I'll just bet," the waitress said.

Charley's eyes narrowed. He walked back to the counter and spread a quarter, dime and a nickel next to the plate.

Out in the street he headed for Wisconsin Avenue. The din of the city muffled the sound of his wooden heels on the concrete. The acrid odors of auto exhausts stung his eyes, his nostrils. He looked up toward the sun, but it was only a lemon disc almost invisible through the shroud of smog.

He walked all morning, hardly knowing where. Several times people called out to him. If he saw them he gave no sign.

At noon he was at the lakefront where the roar of Lake Michigan's surf competed with the roar of autos along Lake Shore Drive.

He stood looking out to where an ore boat trailed a long plume of black smoke. Then as he was turning away someone had him by the arm.

"Charley! Charley! We need you. Where've you been?"

He looked at the man. Though he recognized him, he could not put a name to the face.

"Come on," the man urged, pulling at his sleeve. "Come on. We need every Bow-and-Arrow in Milwaukee. It's time we showed them."

Charley wondered if the man knew that only yesterday they had buried his mother. Obviously not, because he was propelling him along Lake Shore Drive, talking as he walked. "We're going to hold out," he said. "Nothing'll make us move. It's our one big chance to show them all that we mean business."

Charley remembered. Three Indian families, to protest inadequate and substandard housing, had barricaded themselves in an abandoned United States Coast Guard station. The station was now cordoned off by a solid wall of Indians, whites and a scattering of blacks.

Many of his friends had become involved. Some had tried to involve him. He had refused as he had many times before, believing as had his mother that it was the wrong way.

"We must work from within the system," she had said. "We only exhaust ourselves, create ill will, defeat our purpose by going around breaking windows."

Sometimes he wondered, what had it availed her to work from within the system? She was qualified to be a school principal, yet they had relegated her to being a fifth-grade teacher.

Sometimes seeing the doubt in her son's eyes, she had said, "Of course it's not right, Charley. It's wrong. But the other way is wrong too. You don't fight evil with evil. Not ever."

More and more Charley had come to question her position. What had it gotten him? Part-time work in a gas station? Was that his reward? Six months, the longest he'd ever held one job, handling

4

dynamite for an explosives expert who worked for the Army Corps of Engineers. Was that the ultimate, the most he could ever expect? That, and a week washing dishes here, a week parking cars? Damn it, what had he profited by not breaking windows?

Charley was still walking with the man who had him by the elbow. Rounding a curve in the drive, he could see the Coast Guard station and rank upon rank of men, women and children locked together, arm in arm.

"We're just in time," the man said, beginning to jerk the boy along as he ran. "The fight's about to start."

Charley held back. He was not ready, not for this. The man jerked his arm. "You going to show the white feather? You going to let those bastards scalp your friends, your people?"

Charley went along.

"Over here!" the man urged. "The back way!"

They went along the beach to where the mooring slip presented a bulwark of concrete, and then into the water quickly, around the boats in dry dock, up the sloping beach, right into a charge the police were making to break up and disperse the crowd.

Momentarily the crowd, linked by hand and arm holds, held their ground. Then their line of defense began to waver. Charley, still held loosely by the man whose name he still couldn't remember, began to hold back. But it was already too late. The line of protesters broke and the police swarmed through. With clubs swinging, uniformed police and plainclothesmen pushed the protesters back. Those who resisted were clubbed to the ground. In sharp contrast to the undisciplined ranks of the protesters, the police coordinated their efforts. Squads of officers surrounded and broke off segments of picketers one at a time and herded them back toward a chain fence where retreat was impossible.

Charley saw two plainclothesmen and one uniformed officer snap handcuffs on two men who had been near him, and chain them to the fence. As the three policemen turned to seek out other victims rocks began to fly. A uniformed police officer went down, blood spreading over his forehead. Charley stood aghast. Then he looked around frantically, dropped his suitcase and turned, hoping to lose himself in the crowd. He saw two men come toward him. He started to run but it was too late. The two plainclothesmen had him.

An overwrought uniformed officer joined them and slammed him across the stomach with a night stick. He bent double, gasping for air.

"What's your name, kid?" someone asked. But Charley could not speak. "I asked you, what's your name?" the man repeated, jostling him.

Charley gasped, "Nightwind. Charley Nightwind."

He was being dragged forward to where men were kneeling around the prostrate figure. One of them looked up. He pointed a finger, and then he said, "Well, this time you did it, kid. This time you did it. He's dead."

Shots rang out. Out of the corner of his eye, Charley saw two Indians fall. One was a child. He turned and tried to free himself. He felt a club across his kidneys. "Not so fast. You're not going anywhere!"

Some other officers came up. "Who did it? Which one?"

They pointed at Charley. It was then the boy realized that they were accusing him of a killing. "Get him out of here," someone shouted. Then they prodded him with night sticks and fists, and first one then another, called him a killer.

They were almost to the car when suddenly there was a circle of silence and the group parted to permit an officer wearing sergeant's chevrons to step up.

"This the guy?"

"It's him, all right."

Charley heard the man mutter beneath his breath, "Savage bastards." Then the sergeant turned to one of the men who had a wrist lock on him. "Well, read him his rights, and don't wait for the wagon. Just get him on up to the station. Fast! And try not to kill him on the way."

Someone began to chant, and Charley heard only snatches of what he was saying: ". . . you have the right to remain silent . . . anything you say may be . . . you have the right to . . . a lawyer . . ."

Then quite precipitously he was in the back seat of the police car sandwiched between two plainclothesmen, the siren screaming in his ears. As the car careened out of the parking lot, Charley thought he saw two other autos speeding toward it.

They drove up Wisconsin Avenue and met an ambulance speeding east toward the lakefront.

Storefronts whisked by. People crowded the curb to wait, and look as they passed by.

One of the plainclothesmen turned to look out of the rear window. "We've got company," he said.

"How many?" the officer to Charley's left asked.

"Two, I think."

"Well, we'd better get cuffs on this guy. Mine are back holding some bastards to the fence. Got yours?"

"Mine are alongside yours, doing the same thing."

"Makes no difference," the man on the left said. "I hope he makes a break for it. It'll be a good excuse to fix his wagon."

Charley looked straight ahead at the back of the neck of the uniformed driver. The plainclothesman to his right looked back again. "One of the cars has turned off," he said. "They may be circling to try to cut us off."

"Let them come," the other man said, pulling a submachine gun from a canvas scabbard fastened to the door of the car.

The police car driver slowed the vehicle to make a right turn toward Wells Street. Several blocks down the street loomed the high white Safety Building which housed the police department.

Then, quite suddenly, like a burst of judgment, an auto came hurtling from an alley to strike the squad car broadside, sending it careening down the street to wheel over on its side.

When the boy's mind struggled back from

the screech of rending metal, the smell of burning oil, the shouts and cries of pain . . . he was lying sprawled in the gutter. Instinctively he tried to sink lower, as if to bury himself from sight. Then recognizing the futility of such a maneuver, he was on his feet and running.

Behind him he heard someone shout, heard a shot, and thought he heard a bullet whine. He never looked back, but ran down the alley out of which the offending vehicle had come to crack open the squad car spilling its cargo along the street. He hurdled garbage cans, sent one rattling. Then at Sixth Street he turned north—still running. People moved out of his way, watching. Soon the air burned in his lungs and his legs began to tire. His head pounding, he dashed up another alley, and exhausted slipped to his knees in a doorway.

When Charley Nightwind was breathing normally again, he got up and went unhurriedly back out into the street and continued north. No one tried to stop him. He glanced behind. No one was in pursuit. Where a high fence guarded acres of auto hulks, he stood warily watching the street. When the street was clear, he climbed the fence, and dropping inside the junk yard, scrambled swiftly, like a hunted animal seeking safety in this jungle of steel.

In an old Oldsmobile a frayed back seat offered him a place to rest. Gradually then, it dawned on him that in one frightful second, at the instant the rock had been thrown, his entire life had changed. But this time there was no one, not a living person he could go to now that his mother was dead.

2

From high on a hill Charley Nightwind looked down on Spirit Flowage. Moonlight was on the water which spread in all directions like silver web strands spun by a bewildered spider.

The trek north had been an arduous one, but it had been the only direction he could go—toward the land of his fathers—the Lost Nation Indian Reservation.

Under cover of darkness he had left the city. He had hopped a freight train, but abandoned it when the tracks turned west. He then accepted a ride from a truck driver who was headed north. Sleeping in woodlots by day, and hiking at night, he had come at last to the land of tall trees and many waters.

Now he was back to the place where he'd been born. Though he had lived here for the first five years of his life, he had no recollection of it. There were only the secondhand memories of his mother— stories heavy with sorrow.

"We were a throw-away people," she had said, "assigned to live in a throw-away place."

She had said nothing to prepare him for the beauty of these waterways, a great man-made lake with a hundred or more islands, half of them floating free.

Instead she had called it a place of exile. Sometimes, with tears swimming in her eyes, she'd slip an arm around his shoulders and say, "Don't go back there. It's a trap, because that is what it was meant to be: A place to die, but no place to live."

She had never mentioned the deer which came to drink, the air like clear glass, and this moonlight, white as lightning. Why? he wondered. When the city was so dirty, so noisy, so foul. Why hadn't she told him about the scarlet maples? The oak leaves of burnished copper? Never any of these. Only tales of woe, of unbelievable blizzards. Of snow for cauterizing the flow of blood at childbirth. Days in bed just to keep from freezing. Desperate men numb for weeks with whiskey. Rice and more rice, until it congealed, lumped in the throat. These were the things she had told him about.

Being a schoolteacher, he supposed, had given her a sharp focus of the deplorable world—as she had called it—of the American Indian. She would quote statistics: Infant mortality rate three times that of the rest of the country. Longevity? An Indian dead at forty-four—a white man lived almost until seventy. And the teen-agers. "They have no

11

hope," she had said. "Their suicide rate is three times that of all other children."

Perhaps, if his father had lived, his life might have been different. Charley Nightwind gazed at the land below. Down there somewhere, down where the rolling forest crest was luminescent, a falling tree had finished him.

Charley tried to shake the past and step back into the moonlight which was working its magic all around him. It must have been nearly midnight, but he wasn't tired. Ever since he'd fled the city to come some three hundred miles to this place of his beginning, he had not needed much sleep, and though he had eaten only intermittently, he wasn't hungry.

He walked in the dry grass until he came to the crest of a ridge. The sign he was looking for was there:

BURIAL GROUND

He followed the trail and came to another clearing with a scattering of wood crosses, and here and there markers of stone, with occasional graves fenced in and roofed over with boards. Protection against what? Rain? Sun? Evil Spirits? He didn't know.

He stood for a while looking out over the Burial Ground. But no spirits, as he had half expected, came to hover wraith-like above the graves. He knelt then beside a cross to read the inscription which had been burned into the wood:

BRIGHT MORNING STAR

ONLY SIX—1898—SMALLPOX

12

Another marker nearby was a field stone shot through with silver threads of mica. "A good Man," was all it said.

The next grave was new.

A small marble marker, a gravestone company product, read:

CLARA CLEARWATER
1921   1974

He hadn't realized that the Burial Ground was still used. He had thought it held only the remains of those who had died fifty or more years ago. At that time, the old reservation burial grounds were moved to prevent flooding by the newly completed power company dam.

The next cross was down. As he picked it up the wood crumbled in his fingers. He turned it so the light of the moon was full on it. All he could make out was the name, "Eagleclaw." The rest was unreadable. He gently laid the cross back down.

And so he went from grave to grave, up one row and down the other; kneeling at times, or lifting a cross in the moonlight to read the marking.

In the last row he found what he was looking for. The marker had almost sunk from sight. He might have missed it if his boot hadn't grazed the moss revealing the dull shine of metal. They had said it was copper.

He dropped to his knees, and with his pocketknife scraped away earth and moss and a few tiny plants, digging all around until the copper marker stood in relief.

He sat beside the marker rubbing it gently

with his bare hands until letters began to appear. Gradually the inscription on the marker began to materialize:

CHIEF CHARLEY NIGHTWIND
SHOT 1924 AT THE DAM SITE

He had not known about the killing. All they'd told him was that his grandfather was buried on the hill, and that the bodies of all the Indians had been moved from the Old Burial Ground to the hill. That was all they had told him.

He moved further along until he found his father's grave. John Nightwind. Carved on fieldstone. Charley Nightwind sat down, in the moonlight in the clearing, home among the dead of his people.

He recalled the day more than eight years ago, when he was only a boy. That day, he had stood on the edge of an excavation in downtown Milwaukee where a high-rise apartment was scheduled to go up. He looked down, watching three men in the pit sorting out bones.

One of the men had looked up at him and nudged the other men.

"Think some of these might be your relatives?" the man said.

At first Charley hadn't understood. He watched as the men continued sorting out the skeletons—two shinbones to a pile, one skull to a pile, two arm bones to a pile. It wasn't until he was back in his mother's apartment that it dawned on him that the three men had uncovered an ancestral graveyard and were sorting out Indian bones.

14

3

With a sigh Charley Nightwind turned his back on the Burial Ground and came once more to the road which wound down the hill into the valley. He was tiring now, for the first time since starting north four days ago. Perhaps now, in the serenity of the forest he was relaxing—something he hadn't been able to do during his flight.

In the valley he passed houses of unpainted boards and they were silver-gray in the moonlight. Dogs barked as he passed, and some came out to sniff him, the hair on their backs bristling.

At last he came back to Donny Strong's home. He had stopped there briefly on his way to the Burial Ground, because a woman at the trading post had said, "He's the man to see if you're coming to live on the reservation."

So he knew about the dog which slept in the

lean-to attached to the house, and he whistled softly. The dog, of collie-like proportions, came and stood at his knee. "Nice fella," Charley said, scratching behind the dog's ears. The dog wagged his thanks, and together they went quietly around to the back of the house.

The dog went into the lean-to and Charley followed. Just inside the door he stopped. The commingling of odors was stifling. Deer hides, salted and rolled, had once laid here too long. Here smoked fish, hanging from hooks, had left their smell, and there were skunk fumes and the odor of mink and weasel musk from pelts cured there and now long sold. There was the odor of urine let in lazy moments, and on icy nights which made a trip to the outhouse too much of an ordeal.

Charley began to gag and backed out. Outside he breathed deeply to rid his lungs of the foul air. Then he walked a little way and crawled into an opening wedge at the base of a large hemlock and, like an animal, curled up and fell asleep.

The boy slept soundly until the sun began to filter light through the trees. Then the dog nudged him awake. He rubbed his eyes and shivered. Smoke was pouring from the black stovepipe on the roof of the house.

He got up, looked toward the outhouse, but went around back of the tree instead. Then with the dog leading the way, he went around to the front of the house and knocked at the door.

"Who's there?" It was a startled query.

"Only me. Charley."

"Oh." Silence. "Well, come on in."

16

Donny, a squat man with a round, unwrinkled face and short black hair, stood naked to the waist feeding poplar splits into a black old-fashioned stove.

"Did you find it, the Burial Ground?" Donny asked. Charley nodded.

In the center of the room where the Indian was building up the fire stood a square, rough-hewn table. A kerosene lamp with a blackened chimney stood in the middle of what obviously were last night's supper dishes. A half-dozen straight-backed, unpainted chairs stood around as if not knowing which way to face. And blankets were piled up in one corner and under them the Old Woman he had caught sight of earlier stirred, coming awake.

A voice came down the open stairway from the loft. "Who is it, Donny?"

"It's only Charley."

"Oh."

"Come on down and help me get the Old Woman up."

"I'm tired."

"Teersa!"

"Okay."

Charley felt awkward. "I'll take a walk," he said, looking off at the smoke-yellowed print on the wall which had once been the bright shining picture of a woman in a flower garden.

"You don't have to."

"I'd rather."

"Okay. We'll eat in half-an-hour."

Charley went out the door. The dog was waiting. Through the tree trunks he could see water and he followed the trail that took him to a beach. He stood for a while feeling the sun on his face, looking out where the floating islands rode quietly because there was no wind. Glancing about, checking that no one was around, he began to undress.

The icy water of Spirit Flowage took his breath away. He came out after a couple of minutes. As he scrubbed himself with sand from the beach, he noticed a young girl with long black braids carrying a pail. She waded ankle deep and filled the pail. When she turned she saw him and stood still. He turned his back, and when he looked again, she had disappeared among the trees.

He felt better now and walked slowly back to the house, knocked and then went in.

Donny's wife, thinner than her husband, was stirring a kettle of gruel. Her black hair fell in a tangle almost to her skirt. She was barefoot.

"Sit down, Charley. It will be ready in a minute," the man said.

The Old Woman was up too. She was sitting in the only easy chair in the room, a wooden rocker with a dirty pillow for sitting and a stuffed burlap bag sewed into place for a head rest.

"Did you find it?" the Old Woman asked. Her voice was like the rattle of dry reeds.

Charley nodded, but the woman, unable to see across the room, asked again, "Did you find it?"

"I found it."

"Come closer."

Charley walked across the room.

"Closer. Lean down to me."

18

His leg was touching the long, black skirt which hid her feet. Then he leaned forward until his head was only inches from the tiny, bird-black eyes.

"You look like him. You look like Chief Nightwind." The Old Woman sat back, relaxed. "He was the last."

"She's one hundred and five, or so she says," Teersa explained.

Charley looked at the Old Woman again. She was a web of brown wrinkles. Wisps of gray hair stuck out straw-like from beneath the black scarf which covered her head.

"Teersa, when do we eat?" Donny asked impatiently.

"Right now." She set the kettle of gruel, a cup of sugar and a can of condensed milk on the table. Donny switched on a radio, and then the two of them slid the Old Woman's chair across the floor so she could sit at the table. Each took a bowl. Teersa helped the Old Woman. Donny sat down, and motioned for Charley to take a chair. Sugar first, melting on the hot gruel. Milk, yellow streaks in the gray mush. They began eating, the Old Woman slurping from a spoon held in both trembling hands.

Music on the radio softened the sounds of eating. "Lay your head upon my pillow . . ." Soft love song. Warm love song. Love song of some other place.

The music stopped, and the announcer cut in: "We have a news bulletin from Milwaukee. The search for Charley Nightwind, alleged killer of Police Officer Patrick Walsh, has shifted north. Officials believe he might have fled to the Lost

Nation Indian Reservation in northwestern Wisconsin's Birnamwood County."

Only the Old Woman kept on eating. The others at the table fell silent.

4

"You can't stay here," Donny said. "When there's trouble, one of the first places they check is the house of Donny Strong. It's been like that ever since the thing of the dam."

The Old Woman, being helped back into bed by Teersa, caught the one word, "dam."

"That's where they killed him. Down by the dam," she muttered.

Charley glanced at her. "What is she talking about?"

"About your grandfather. You see, he was the chief," Teersa said. Charley looked surprised.

"She remembers that clearly," Donny added. "Fifty years ago the Chippewas fought the state, the federal government and the Power Company to prevent them from erecting a dam across Spirit River." He looked away from Charley, and speaking more softly continued, "Your grandfather and four other men were killed." He hesitated, then nodded toward the Old Woman. "Fifty years ago," he went on, "only she thinks it was yesterday that the old bones in the Burial Ground were dug up, moved, carried high up onto the hill out of reach of the water."

Donny paused. For a moment then his eyes sparked angrily. "Moving the dead was a stroke of genius," Donny continued after a long pause. "The newspapers across the country ate it up. They said it was a great and noble thing the government was doing, to move the Burial Ground. But they never wrote a line about the fields of squash which went underwater, about the destruction of thousands of acres of wild rice which the people depended on, about the forests of maple from which they got syrup to sell in the cities. All they wrote and talked about was the gathering up of the old bones, moving them to a new Burial Ground."

Charley didn't understand. "But that was fifty years ago. How does that involve you today?"

"The Power Company's lease was for fifty years. It expires in three months. They want a new fifty-year lease. We've been opposing it. We want the dam destroyed, the Flowage drained, so we can go back to the land which has always been and still is ours," Donny explained.

"And you've been . . ." Charley never finished the sentence. A car had driven up, stopped on the road in front of the house. Donny darted to a window.

"It's Chauncey Gambrel, the game warden. Out the back door!"

Charley ran out past the dog, and on down the trail into the forest.

Inside the house Donny let the warden rap four times before answering the door. "Can I come in?" the warden asked.

"You will anyway," Donny said.

The Old Woman grabbed her black shawl and pulled it up over her head.

The warden walked past Donny and stood looking around. He was wearing a uniform of gray-green twill, a gold-and-green shoulder patch, and there was no hat on his head of red hair.

"We're looking for Charley Nightwind. You seen him?"

Beneath the black shawl the Old Woman stirred. "Chief Nightwind is dead. They killed him down at the dam," she said.

"What's that?" the warden asked, nodding toward the pile of rumpled blankets on the bed.

"Fifty years ago Chief Nightwind was killed by sheriff's men. . . ."

"A man named Nightwind was killed at the dam site?" the warden asked.

Donny nodded.

The warden stepped toward where the Old Woman lay and moved a hand as though to take the black shawl from her face. "Why does she keep covered?" he asked.

"In fifty years she has never looked at a white

man, and in fifty years she has never let a white man look at her. Ever since the thing of the dam. It's her way of protesting."

"I ought to jerk that black rag off her," the warden said.

"You do and I'll kill you," Donny said.

The warden turned abruptly to stare at Donny. "Just make sure," he said, "that it isn't I who kill you." The warden walked to the steps which led to the loft. "Is he up there?"

"Is who up there?" Donny stalled.

"Charley Nightwind."

"It's like the Old Woman said. Charley Nightwind was killed fifty years ago at the dam."

The warden turned to face Donny. "That's what you say."

"That's what *I* say," Donny said. "And anyway, by what right are you on the reservation? By what right are you in my home? Please get out."

The warden laughed. "Before the day is over, you'll be having plenty of company. Cops don't take kindly to cop killers."

"I don't know what you're talking about."

"You're a liar!"

Hearing the word "liar," the Old Woman spoke: "If you call me a liar again I'll call Charley Nightwind to throw you out. Charley Nightwind is here. He's come back."

"See," Teersa said, "I told you she doesn't know what she's talking about. She's one hundred and five years old."

Another car had driven up, and within seconds the door burst open and a tall, heavy man

24

wearing a brown uniform with yellow stripes down the side of the trousers, walked in. "Anything?" he asked, talking to the warden.

"I think he was here, Sheriff. The Old Woman spilled the beans."

"How long ago?" the sheriff asked.

"Not long."

"What do you suggest?"

"Well that's within your jurisdiction. I just rode out here on a hunch, but maybe you'd better take this couple in. They might talk."

Teersa took a step forward. "We can't leave the Old Woman. She's helpless."

"Maybe just the man then," the warden suggested.

"You got a warrant?" Donny asked.

"We can get one," the sheriff said.

"And what would you charge me with?"

"Accessory after the fact. Harboring a fugitive. Maybe disorderly conduct. You name it. If you're choosey you can have your pick. We aren't particular."

Teersa dropped a tin plate. It clattered on the board floor.

"Is that Charley Nightwind come back?" the Old Woman asked. "Give him the rifle. It shoots farther than the shotgun."

"See what I mean," the warden said, turning to the sheriff.

"Yeah, he was here all right."

"Maybe a posse," the warden suggested.

"We'd need a hundred men. They'd be shooting one another."

"Well, he's got to come out for food."

"Maybe not. Some of these Bow-and-Arrows can live on grass and tree bark," the sheriff said.

"Not this one," the warden smirked. "He's a city Indian. Never been off concrete in his life."

The sheriff shook his head. "There's a hundred homes to watch. It'd take too many men."

"What then?"

"Dogs, I think."

"But where can you get hounds that will trail a man?"

"A guy over in Minneapolis."

"How long would it take to get them here?" the warden asked.

"If we call now, they could fly them over in less than an hour."

"Then what are we waiting for?"

As they started toward the door, the sheriff nodded at the Old Woman. "What's with her?" he asked. "Why does she keep her head covered?"

Teersa explained again.

"Crazy," the sheriff said, and went through the door. The warden followed him out.

The voice of the Old Woman broke the silence in the house. "I hope I live long enough. Tell Charley Nightwind to hurry," she said. Then she lifted the black shawl from her face.

5

Charley Nightwind ran straight for the Flowage shore. There he followed the beach, staying back among the trees. The spit of land narrowed. Shortly he saw water on either side. He was on a peninsula which narrowed down to a needle point of scattered rock with a huge, black boulder at the tip. He went around to the sunny side of the big rock and sank down on the warm stones.

Now he was tired. The anxious week seemed to fall—all at once—like an avalanche on his spirit. He lay back, done in. He closed his eyes. The warm sun was a caress of comfort, and in a very few minutes, without meaning to, he fell asleep.

He woke with a start. A girl was standing over him, a forefinger to her lips. "Shhhh. Be quiet," she said softly.

He sat up abruptly. It was the girl who had come for water and had seen him standing naked on the beach.

"You can't stay here," she said. "You've got to get off the peninsula. They've got you trapped."

Charley hunched forward, taking in the girl, the sandals, the blue jeans, the flowered blouse, the large brown eyes. When she glanced away he let his eyes move across her honey cheeks, to the little nose and the purple-red mouth.

"You are Charley Nightwind, aren't you?" she asked. He nodded. "I'm Betty Sands."

"Oh?" It was all he could think of to say.

"You've got to get out of here. They're coming."

"But, how do they know I'm here?"

"Listen."

Charley listened and heard only the sound of water among the rocks.

"The dogs. Don't you hear them?"

Now he heard dogs. "They are far away," he said.

"Not really. They're coming down the peninsula."

"Then I can't go back?"

"No. There are twenty or more men and two dogs. You'd never get through. If you run, they'll shoot you, kill you."

Charley looked out over the coppery water. Two hundred yards away one of the bog islands floated.

"Can you swim?" the girl asked. Charley

nodded. "Well then, perhaps you'd better, because you can't stay here."

Charley turned to look back among the trees in the direction of the dogs. "There's not much time," the girl said. Once more he looked up at her. Then he pulled off his leather boots.

"You'll need them," the girl said, and whipping a red bandana from her head, she bundled the boots. "Tie them around your neck," she said.

Charley got up and did as she suggested. He looked at the girl. "Do your folks live here?"

She nodded. "Not far from Donny Strong."

"Have you lived on the reservation long?"

"All my life." She dropped her eyes and looked at the ground. When she looked up again, she asked, "Did you kill a policeman?"

"No."

"They say you did."

"There was a fight. The police were trying to evict some Indian families from an abandoned Coast Guard station. They claim I threw the rock that killed the cop."

"Did you throw a rock?" the girl asked.

"No."

"Who did kill the policeman?"

"I don't know. A lot of people were throwing rocks."

"If you didn't kill the policeman, why don't you give yourself up. If you run, they'll think for sure you did it."

Charley Nightwind shook his head. "No. Someone is going to prison. They've decided it's

29

going to be me. I'd rather be dead than locked up."

The sound of the dogs came loudly now on a turn of the wind, and the girl looked at him squarely. "You've got to go. They'll be here in ten minutes. Make the sound of a loon. That'll be the signal. When I hear it, I'll bring food." She turned away then, and disappeared silently down the trail.

The sound of a loon? He had never heard a loon, so how could he make the sound of a loon?

Now the baying of the dogs was only a drumbeat away. Charley entered the water, then lunged forward and began a swift, silent swim toward the floating island.

Betty Sands ran on the trail for a short distance, and then turned abruptly from it. She skirted briar patches, leaped over logs, and crossed windfalls with the dexterity of a squirrel. Near the beach she turned and headed straight for the dogs, now visible among the trees.

She heard a man shout, "It's only a girl." Then the dogs were upon her, tails whipping, long tongues dripping saliva, jumping so their pendulous ears flapped ludicrously. She dropped to her knees, and the dogs, exuberant at such attention, permitted her arms around their necks.

"Hey, what the hell you think you're doing?" a man shouted.

Wide-eyed, feigning innocence, Betty looked up into the face of the sheriff, and said, "I meant only to help. I thought you were trying to catch the dogs."

The sheriff's face turned red. "You're a liar," he said. "Let those dogs go!"

Other men came through the brush. "What the hell's happening?" one asked.

"This squaw," the sheriff fumed, "is impeding justice."

A lean, leathery man stepped out from the circle of men which had closed around the girl. He snapped leather leads to the collars of both animals and dragged them back. The girl stood up.

"I'm sorry if I spoiled your hunting party," she said.

"I'll just bet you are," the sheriff snorted. "Now where's that damned kid? Tell us if you want to stay out of trouble."

"The kid?" Betty's brow wrinkled into a look of perplexity.

The warden stepped forward. "That's Betty Sands," he said. "You won't get anything from her. There's no use trying. We've got him trapped. All we have to do, is move on down the peninsula and keep an eye open so he doesn't slip between us."

The men fanned out then to put a cordon across the peninsula. The sheriff gave Betty a parting shot, "We're not through with you. We'll be back." Betty waited until they had disappeared among the trees. Then she went back to the trail and followed quietly inland to where the peninsula widened.

The dogs, held in check now, were silent. The men made no attempt to conceal their progress through the brush. One or another, from time to time, cursed vehemently as a limb or a deadfall or a bramble patch impeded his progress.

At the tip of the peninsula they came together in a knot of sweating bodies. The hounds waded into the water lapping eagerly, their long ears half-submerged.

"What do you think?" the sheriff asked, turning to the warden.

"Probably swam to the island."

All the men looked out toward the island. It was drifting away from the shore on which they stood. The two smaller islands which flanked it were also moving.

"He could move from one island to another forever," one of the men said. "It would be like looking for a weasel in a stone pile. Move one stone and it ducks under another."

The sheriff turned to the warden, "What do you think?"

"I don't know. If, as you say, he's a Sidewalk Indian maybe we can get him. If he was one of the reservation Indians he'd know how to use the islands, and you'd never get him."

"Let's get boats," the warden said, turning away and starting back down the trail which led off the peninsula. The others followed in single file.

Shortly after noon Betty heard the snarl of motors in the distance. She ran out of the house, and down the peninsula trail. Shielding her eyes from the sun she saw gleaming boats zeroing in from every direction.

The island to which Charley Nightwind had swam, was far out now, standing motionless up against an underwater reef. Five boats began to circle the island, coming closer on each swing. First one and then another of the boats pushed up against the boggy shores as the posse prepared for an assault.

The swim to the island so tired Charley that, for a while, he could merely hang there in the water, his elbows on the boggy shore, his legs floating behind him.

When the thumping of his heart subsided, he climbed up on the trembling earth and crept across until he was screened by the dark green vegetation. Propping himself up on his elbows, he parted the rushes in time to see the posse converge around the big rock on the tip of the peninsula.

It gave him an eerie feeling to be on the island; nothing more than a quaking network of roots woven from thousands of plants. No wonder they called it Spirit Flowage. The fragile island was moving, and there was something almost ghost-like in sailing slowly along on a green acre which even supported scattered groves of stunted tamarack trees.

Moving toward the center of the island, Charley saw a creature flee like a dark shadow. He did not recognize the lance of fur because he had never seen a mink. Here too there was a muskrat house, high dome of coontail moss thatched with rushes. And though he knew what it was from pictures and having read about muskrats, it was the first such den he had ever seen.

It was like that with most of the flora and fauna, so he didn't know that the plant with the tough leaves which sometimes contrived to trip him up, was called leather leaf. And though he recognized the eagle searching the sky for thermal drafts to glide upon, it was the first such bird he had ever seen.

Exhausted and frightened as he was, Charley marveled at his surroundings. He had often talked about visiting the reservation, but his mother had always said, "You go back and you'll find nothing. Nothing except poverty. Poverty and ignorance. Poverty cutting just enough pulp wood to keep you alive. Poverty hunting, trapping and fishing where there's little left to hunt, trap or fish for."

Still, at unpredictable times—while walking in a park, standing between the concrete canyons looking up at the scudding clouds, coming to the lakefront where gulls and ducks skimmed the waves —he experienced a heart tug for which he had no explanation.

Boots still tied in the scarf around his neck, Charley crossed to the end of the island, lowered himself into the water and began to swim slowly toward another island floating a couple hundred yards away. His knee came up sharply against an underwater obstruction. Searching with his bare feet, he found the limb of an old treetop still standing, though the waters had backed over it fifty years ago. He looked down through the coppery water. He could see the dim outline of the branches, grotesque like the bony fingers of a reaching skeleton. He stood on the highest limb and it raised him halfway out of the water so he could rest.

A few moments later, he continued swimming. Again his legs grazed the tops of still standing trees, and then he was levering himself out onto the watery bog he intended to use as a place of refuge.

The island was smaller than the one he had left. It had but a single tiny tamarack, but was lush with other vegetation. He crawled until he came to the single tamarack, and then, like an animal, flattened a bed for himself by rolling in the leather leaf.

Then, even before he heard the distant snarl of outboard motors, the island jarred to a shivering halt, and he guessed it had become snagged on some underwater obstruction—a tree or a reef—and was now anchored.

Several islands drifted by, and then he noticed that some other islands had also anchored, and were holding a steady place in the Flowage.

From time to time he lifted his head from his animal nest in the leather leaf to watch the boats converge on the island he had just left.

Well, he thought, when they finished with

that island, they'd have a choice of plenty others, several of which had now drifted in between him and his pursuers.

There were fifty—or was it a hundred—islands, and unless they were lucky, and so long as he kept moving from place to place, it was conceivable he might elude them if his strength held out.

Though he tried to stay awake, the long swim and the sleepless days and nights of the preceding week of flight, now combined to induce a comforting lethargy. For a few seconds, he thought to resist, but then the luxury of succumbing to sleep was too inviting; he closed his eyes, and surrendered.

It was midday and warm for the first week in October. Above him a gray deerfly circled warily and then dived and fastened its savage little mouth on his bare ankle. In his sleep, Charley shuddered, and kicked the fly away.

The sound of his breathing was less than the sound of the breeze among the rushes, and a gangling green heron, its gullet distended with fish, came clumsily into the tip of the single, small tamarack. The boy never heard the tentative squawk, or the rustle of wing feathers.

The boats were leaving the island where he had first sought refuge. The heron watched them as they cruised in circles until one suddenly arrowed toward another island, and then in single file the others trailed along.

So the afternoon went slowly for the glutted bird, and for the boy curled up in the leather leaf. The posse moved methodically from island to island, and if the heron could have counted, it would have known there were seven boats and eighteen men. But, of course, if the heron had recognized the slumbering figure below in the leather leaf as that of a human, it would never have perched so close in the first place.

This is what the men of the posse thought too. They thought that since the bird sat so quietly in the tiny tamarack, that the island must be deserted. So they passed it up, went on to other islands, and when the sound of their motors began to diminish, the heron folded its brightly striped neck back against its brown body. Its transparent lids, like sheaths of plastic, slipped down over the bird's eyes, and then the outer lids came down too, and the heron slept in the warm October sun, out there on the leather-leaf island which was rocking gently like a flat, green barge on the water of Spirit Flowage.

So the afternoon droned peacefully toward evening, and when the sun finally touched the rim of trees which surrounded the Spirit Flowage, the heron opened its eyes. The fish had long been digested, and cocking the elbows of its wings, stretching its neck, lifting the abrupt little tail, it discharged a long stream of lime among the branches, whitening the feathery green filament of lacy-like needles.

Then it fluffed its feathers, shook, and when its wings had been tucked back into place, it craned its neck, and launched itself into awkward, hesitating flight.

The sound of wings awakened Charley Nightwind. He opened his eyes, but instinctively lay still until his mind had time to catch up, sort out preceding events, bring him up-to-date on the time and place of his predicament.

The bitter struggle of his recent Milwaukee days now seemed like a distant dream. The precipitous flight north was hardly a thread of remembering. The posse, the dogs, Donny and Teersa Strong, the Old Woman . . . like characters from an old television movie, only dimly seen, almost faceless now.

Only Betty Sands stood out sharply in his mind. The soft-bronze features, the black hair tied with bright ribbons into two braids were near and clear.

He wondered where she was. And how did a loon call? He searched for a clue among old television shows, old movies of wild places. A loon? What bird? And how did it sound?

It grew dark before he gave up. The evening star had been hung out. Here and there, first one star and then another, first dimly seen, and then quickly brightening.

His stomach made a startling sound. He put a hand to it, felt the gut muscles writhe. Water was never enough. He was hungry now for the first time since he'd trudged the long way from Milwaukee's East Side to the western city limits, and then began the long hitchhike north.

With the darkness came life of a different dimension. A horned owl served raucous notice that the hunt would now begin. Soft sound of fur, gliding from land to make a soft splash. Otter? Mink? Muskrat? Beaver? How could he, a Sidewalk Indian, know?

He stood up, bent his knees slightly when the island trembled, straightened them again when he did not go through. Beyond the vague outlines of other islands, he could dimly see a distant shore where tall trees cut a ragged black crest against a sky now brightening with stars.

Should he swim? Try for the shore? Then look for the road back to Donny Strong's house?

It would mean food. He'd get advice. Then he could decide whether to hide out here, in this place, or whether it would be wiser to move on, move north, across Michigan's Upper Peninsula. Cross the Canadian border at Sault Ste. Marie. Keep pushing to where roads ended. Then keep going until he was in the land of the Cree. But would they hide him?

Getting up again he walked to the tiny tamarack, felt around for the bandana holding his boots, slung them around his neck, and went back to the water. Out of the night came a forlorn, lonely wail that took his breath away.

Human? Never. But what in the world? . . . Of course! From some distant recollection, perhaps heard when he was very young, and now echoing down through the years, he remembered: The cry of a loon!

He knew it positively. But he didn't know if it was really a loon, or if it was Betty Sands. He would wait a moment and see. The stars shifted west and a breeze came off the land to riffle the water, then he heard it again, lifting eerily—plaintive, pleading.

He didn't wait now, but cleared his throat and cupping his hands around his mouth, he tried to reproduce the sound. First a failure. Guttural noise. Again. Starting low and slow, lifting, he let out a wail. Then he waited. There! There was his answer. Nearer. Clearer. Ringing.

He answered. Waited. Called again. Then he saw the bow of a small canoe shape up out of the night, and soon a voice: "Are you there, Charley Nightwind?"

When he stepped in, the canoe rocked, almost tipped. "Down on your knees," Betty whispered.

He sank to his knees and the canoe stopped trembling. "Never stand," the girl said, and then repeated, "never stand."

Charley Nightwind couldn't ever remember having been in a canoe before. He knew that he had been, however, because his mother had said that when he was very young his father had wrapped him warmly and taken him along on the trapline.

"He skinned muskrats as he took them from the traps," she said, "and sometimes by the time he got back you'd lie there in the bow of the canoe almost covered with pelts."

Now the canoe glided quietly across the waters, brightened only by the starry reflection from the sky. Charley wondered, as the girl drove the craft forward with swift, sure, almost silent strokes, how she knew her way in the night, and where were they going?

He was cold now. The night air felt frosty. Leaning back against a thwart, he pulled his socks from his boots and put them on. "Leave your boots off," the girl whispered. "I'm wearing moccasins. Your boots will make a racket against the aluminum bottom."

"Where are we going?" Charley asked.

"To the dam site. Donny Strong is waiting there."

Then there was only the sound of the canoe bow rippling through the water, and the hiss of the sharp-bladed paddle as it knifed in and out of the water. They slipped past island after island, and then as if from somewhere in a far corner of his own mind, the murmur of water grew to a roar. Betty was paddling again, angling the canoe across the current, and Charley could see the narrow catwalk looming darkly above the huge concrete abutments of the dam.

The roar of the water was an all-consuming sound now, and the girl leaned forward to give strength to her paddle thrusts and send the canoe gliding out of the current into a quiet bay. Betty rested the paddle again, let the canoe glide. Then Charley heard her hoot softly like an owl. It was the timorous inquiry of the tiny screech owl, one he was familiar with, since he had heard it in Milwaukee parks.

Almost instantly there was an answer. The girl picked up the paddle and swung the canoe quietly about and angled it toward shore.

When the canoe came to a halt against the bank, the girl said, "You can get out now, but be careful."

Charley braced a hand to each gunwale, moved to the bow, and then a strong hand had him by the arm to help him up and beneath the shadows of the trees. He sank to the ground because his legs were numb from sitting on them, and then he heard Betty, "You can put your boots on now."

He recognized Donny Strong among the shadows. "You hungry?" Donny asked. Charley nodded. "Well we've got food for you back at the fire."

They walked for perhaps five minutes, and then Charley saw a glow of light ahead among the trees. They stopped. The girl gave the sound of the owl. An answer, brief and guarded, came from directly ahead. They walked on, and shortly the trail dipped and in moments they descended into a deep, rocky-like grotto, into a natural kettle formation which the glacier had left and in which now no trees grew.

Indistinct forms around the fire materialized into the figures of five men as they came to the kettle floor. They moved to make room, and when the girl sat, Charley sat down beside her. Then Donny handed him a paper sack.

"Food," he said. Then proffering a red vacuum bottle, he added, "coffee."

Charley took the bag, the vacuum bottle. "Eat," the girl said. "No need to wait." He took a chunk of roast venison and a half a loaf of bread from the bag, and hungrily began to alternate slivers of meat with bites of bread.

Donny made the introductions. There were five besides Donny and the girl. Charley caught the names—Frank, Turlene, Jake, Burt, Wilbur—but not the faces. In the flickering light each face was only a dancing thing of shadows.

"Let's talk about our friend first," Donny was saying.

"What's to talk about?" one of the men hunched around the fire asked.

"Well, how are we going to hide him?"

"Hide him?" someone asked. "I thought we ought to tell him to leave."

"But we just can't turn him out," Donny said.

"He goes," one of the men said. "Already he's brought more law to the reservation than we've had here since I can remember. With him here, and half the lawmen in Wisconsin looking for him, someone is bound to discover our plans for dynamiting the dam."

"But, where can he go?" the girl asked.

"That's his problem," the man said.

"That's a rotten attitude," Donny shot back at the man.

"Maybe," the man said, and Charley looked at him. He was a sharp faced Indian with an eagle beak for a nose.

Donny was talking again. "Your attitude is a

sad one. It's precisely the reason Indians can never get together, the reason they never remain united in solving their common problems."

"Donny's right," the girl interrupted.

"I still think he ought to go," the man said. "If he'd leave, the law would leave. We could get on with it."

For a moment no one spoke. Then the girl asked, "If, after the dam is blown, and you had to run away to Milwaukee to hide, wouldn't you feel good if you knew you could hide out with some Indians there?"

The man did not answer.

"Anyway," the girl was talking again, "what you all forget is that he's a member of the tribe, even though he doesn't live on the reservation. You forget he even has a claim to being chief. Remember his grandfather was a chief, a chief killed trying to dynamite the very dam we want to destroy. Maybe he has a right to sit on our council."

"That's ridiculous," the eagle-beaked one said. "But it's what you might expect when you let a woman in on anything. I say it's crazy to let him into this operation. He's a Sidewalk Indian. He couldn't find his way out of a parsnip patch, much less this forest."

It was true, and nobody knew it better than Charley Nightwind, who by then had stopped eating. "I'll go," he said. "I have no desire to interfere with your plans, and Lord knows, I wouldn't sit as a chief, not under any circumstances."

"But where would you go?" the girl asked.

"North," Charley said, "north into Canada."

"You'd never make it," Donny said.

"So I don't make it. I could still give it a good try."

"They'd nail you at the border."

"Maybe not."

The girl took his hand. "You're going to stay." Then, turning her face back to the fire, she said, "That's the trouble with our people. The Menominees think they're the only tribe with a problem. The Apaches are fighting for what they consider *their* rights. In Florida the Seminoles are convinced they are a nation separate from all other Indian nations, and they go their own way without considering the needs of others. All of them, the Sioux, Ojibwas, what's left of the Huron, the Arapahoes . . . every nation fights a separate battle instead of everybody joining forces. There are nearly a million of us now, but we fight in Texas, in California, in Washington, in Wisconsin . . . from coast to coast a hundred little brush fires instead of uniting in our need for evolving Indian culture with all the benefits our country gives to others."

They were strong words for a girl sitting in council with men, and the fire flickered almost as if the flames had been brushed by the force of her words. "Hummmph! Squaw talk!" the beaked one said.

One of the men reached back and added several small sticks to the fire. The sticks blackened, caught flame and the fire flared.

"Let's take a vote," Donny said.

"It wouldn't be official," the eagle-beaked one said.

"So? You want to let the whole tribe in on our plans?" Donny asked.

"They know anyway."

"Sure they know. But not when and how."

Charley Nightwind had gotten to his feet. "I'll go," he said.

"How far would you get?" the girl asked. Then she answered her own question, "You wouldn't make it out of the woods."

No one talked then, and the flames of the small fire reached out to chase the shadows, but the shadows always came sneaking back.

Finally Donny spoke. "I say we vote." He gathered up seven pebbles and gave one to each. Then he took off his black-felt hat and passed it. "A pebble in the hat is a 'no' vote," he said.

Charley felt the girl's fingers on his wrist as she gently urged him down beside her.

Donny Strong took the hat which had completed its circle and turned it right side up. One pebble fell out.

"He stays," Donny Strong said.

Charley felt the girl's hand close over his. He wanted to thank her, to thank Donny Strong. He was about to say that he'd try to be of as little trouble as he could, when suddenly Donny hissed, "Pssst!"

They all leaned forward listening. Donny suddenly scattered the embers of the fire with his bare hands. Quickly then, like shadows, the five men melted back from where sparks still glowed and disappeared.

Charley waited for instructions. He felt Donny's hand on his arm and followed Donny and Betty along a narrow trail in the forest. Behind he heard the crackling of brush.

"They're rushing the fire," Donny whispered.

"Hurry!" the girl said.

Then from the kettle where the fire had been burning there was a man's voice, "Damn! They got away!"

Charley never knew how far they had hurried along the dim trail. He was breathing hard when they stopped, and he could feel the sharp sting of torn flesh where brambles and thorns had left their marks on his shins, arms, even his cheeks. All three sank to the ground then, on the bank of a swift creek.

The moon had risen, was reaching over the tops of the trees and cast a pale glow over the shallow valley. All three lay on their stomachs and lowered their heads into the creek. Their faces dripping, they sat back. After an interval, Donny said, "I think we should leave you here, Charley. When you've rested, follow the creek. You will come to the Flowage. Swim back out to an island. Maybe they won't go back out to look for you there."

Donny got up and started upstream. When

the girl did not follow, he turned and said, "You coming Betty?"

"No, I'll wait. You go. I'll be along. It's early."

"Just be careful," Donny said.

"I will."

The sound of Donny moving upstream along the creek was so muted that Charley couldn't believe anyone could move so quietly at night through a dense forest. "How does he do it?" he asked the girl.

"Do what?"

"Move without a sound."

The girl hesitated before answering. Then she said, "When you've lived like an animal all your life, you move like an animal—quietly."

"I wish I could."

"You will someday," the girl assured him.

"I don't know."

"I do."

"What makes you think so?"

"If you are a horse, you know how to run like a horse. If you are a wolf, you know how to trail like a wolf. If you are an Indian, you know how to do all these things and many more. It will all come back. There are thousands of years of breeding back of these talents. You do not lose them on concrete."

Charley chuckled. "You believe that?" he asked.

"I believe it."

"Well, I hope you're right."

"I am."

They were silent. The forest around was silent, so silent it seemed the silence must reach to the ends of the earth. "Want something more to eat?" she asked. She had retrieved the bag of bread and meat when they fled the fire and handed it to him.

"Don't you want some?" he asked.

"No, it is for you. I can eat when I get home."

"When are you going?"

"Pretty soon. We'll meet again somewhere tonight to talk about the plans for the dam," she said.

"What good's it going to do you?"

"What good's what going to do?"

"Blowing up the dam. They'll only build another."

"It will put an exclamation mark to our protests. It will serve notice on the Power Company, and the state. It will make them see that we mean business. They will call for a meeting in Madison. Then we can tell them how it was before they put the dam across the Spirit River, before they flooded the land."

"How was it?" Charley asked.

The girl didn't answer right away. She looked off, away, above the trees where the moon was illuminating the sky. Then quietly, her voice almost as soft as the sound of the creek water, she began:

"Of course, I never saw it. My mother, my father never saw it. My grandfather saw it. Your grandfather saw it. A lot of old people still living remember. And maybe the years have colored their memories, but to hear them tell about it, to hear them describe the way it once was, you would almost believe that here it was once like Eden, a perfect paradise."

The girl paused, and Charley asked, "But was it? A paradise, I mean?"

"Well, probably not. But it was as beautiful as it was bountiful. You must remember that when the water backed away from the dam it covered the richest, probably the only rich soil in all this vast forest. The water drowned out 20,000 acres of the finest crop land anywhere. It was all bottom land. Some say cabbages grew as big as bushel baskets. They talk about turnips the size of a man's head. They say a tall man couldn't reach to the top of the corn, and the ears were as big and as round as the forearms of a strong man.

"Everybody farmed, and in the river sloughs there were wild rice beds like you'd never believe. And on the slopes there was wood enough for everything and everyone. And with all this bottom land riches there was plenty left over for the deer, for all the animals and birds, and sometimes the partridge were so thick the people packed them in barrels and preserved them, nobody was ever hungry. An Indian could live like an Indian, and the old ways were observed, and . . ." The girl stopped talking and sighed.

"It does sound like paradise," Charley said, excited.

"Probably more important," the girl continued, "white men rarely if ever came. The reservation was out-of-bounds to them. They were not permitted to hunt or fish here, and it was even illegal for a white man to buy game or fish from an Indian."

"I hope the dam is destroyed," Charley said.

"If it is, it will take years for the sun to once more cure the land so it may again produce in such abundance."

"But someday it will happen?" It seemed Charley was pleading with her to make it happen.

"Yes, perhaps someday," the girl said, with a smile on her lips, "and when that someday comes, the Indians will not have to dance for the tourists. They will not have to buy trinkets from Japan and blot out the message 'made in Japan' so they can pawn them off as Indian handiwork. Maybe then the roads will not be lined with beer cans and whiskey bottles, because maybe then the Indian will have hope."

Charley closed his eyes for a moment and lay back. "I think I'd like to live here if that happens," he said.

"It would be heavenly," the girl said.

"Yes, we could have a cow and some pigs, a garden . . ."

She interrupted him. "*We?*"

Charley didn't realize he had said it. He laughed self-consciously, but without embarrassment. "Well *you* could have a cow, and *I* could have a cow, and *you* could have a garden, and *I* could have a garden. And . . ."

The girl held up a hand. "As long as it's only a dream, as long as it's only make believe anyway," she said, "why not make it 'we.' "

They both laughed quietly, naturally as

leaves rustling in the wind, as naturally as water murmuring around stones, without embarrassment.

Then they grew quiet for a moment. "How come you, a girl, are so deeply involved in this?" Charley then asked.

"Simple," Betty said. "I went to school at Sayward. I've got a typewriter. They needed someone to type their petitions, to type their letters to the legislature, to Congress, to the Bureau of Indian Affairs, to the newspapers . . . and I was the only one who could do it. Gradually I became more and more involved, and then when I saw that surely, unless the tribe took some drastic action, the Power Company would get another fifty-year lease to manufacture power with the dam, I suggested they dynamite it."

"You suggested it?"

"Is that so strange?"

"But you don't seem like a violent person."

"I'm not. But did you ever see a cat fight for her kittens? Well someday I want children, and I'm fighting now so they can eat tomorrow—eat in the Garden of Eden!"

"But why don't you just leave the reservation if living conditions are so terrible. With your typing skill, with your education, your brains, you could find work in Milwaukee."

Betty turned to look at him. "Were you happy there? In Milwaukee?"

"No," Charley said. "No, I wasn't."

"Well, do you think I could be happy there?"

"I suppose not. Not when you have such a dream for this valley. I can see the corn now, so tall in the fields. Tell me about it again. I can't get enough of hearing about it. Tell me what it was that my grandfather died for. Tell me what it was he wanted to save. Tell me what he was shot for. Tell me about it again."

So she talked again, quietly about the sweetness of little golden melons ripening in the warm sun on the black earth; about the deer coming down the low, wooded hills in winter for hay from the stacks built for the milk cows; about wild rice, so heavy headed it bent over the gunwales of the canoes needing only a tap to drop the plump kernels to the canvas below.

She talked about the ducks and the geese which followed the rice boats to pick up the leavings; about the turnips, and how if you carried salt you could pick one solid from a field, and with a piece of bread from a pocket, have a noon-day lunch washed down by the cool, clear spring water of a creek.

"And," she continued, "every basement will be full of fish in cans and jars, and there will be bottles of maple syrup shining as the sun, and there will be sacks of flour, onions and peppers hanging, bins of potatoes, squash and carrots in sand, and there will be whole pigs to be halved, quartered and cut to pan size, and there will be peace and love and warmth."

And she talked about the old men and the old women, and how then, once again, the young would sit at their feet seeking the old wisdom. Finally she was quiet, and for a very, very long time they only sat there beside the little creek, in the deep forest where the moon was laying trails, leaning ever so slightly one against the other, and then Charley Nightwind said softly:

"It could be more than just a dream. We could make it come true. Let me help."

It was almost light by the time Charley came to where the creek stopped arguing noisily with the clustering of rocks and ran quietly to lose itself in the waters of the Flowage.

There was a thin rime of frost, white on the edges of the brown bracken, a dark wetness on the stones which still held a little of yesterday's heat. He sat to pull his boots off, put them in the big paper bag which held what was left of the bread and meat, and entered the water. It was warm, much warmer than the air.

He walked until he was neck-deep in the water, and then turned over on his back, and holding the paper bag high with one hand, he paddled with the other arm and kicked with his legs, and was thus propelled in the direction of the nearest island which loomed like some ghostly barge waiting on a signal from the wind to start moving again.

It had been a long swim to make on his back. He was glad for the opportunity to lie down and rest.

They had parted—he and the girl—sometime after midnight, and he hadn't wanted to leave because he had never felt so fulfilled. But she had insisted. "They will come again in the morning, with the dogs," she had said. The older the trail, the more trouble they will have finding you. Stay in the creek as much as possible. That may fool them for a while."

She had been right. They had come, and with the dogs. As he lay there trying to shiver himself warm, the sky was split apart in the east by a wedge of light, and shortly then he heard the hounds. He crawled to the center of the island for safety. When the sun rose to warm him, he finally fell asleep.

When he awakened the sun was halfway up the sky, but the baying of the hounds was still an infrequent sound as they tried to unravel the devious trail he had laid. He opened the large brown paper bag and ate the rest of the bread and meat, pried apart the roots where he was lying, and when water seeped through he lifted some to his lips with a cupped hand.

Quite suddenly then he heard the hounds line out, bay confidently in a straight run, and he knew they had come to where he had walked the creek bank beside the last stretch of fast water. When they barked sharply in consternation, he knew they were on the beach, at the point where he had walked into the waters of the Flowage.

He stretched out, still sleepy, and with the sun warning him he dozed again until the snarl of approaching motors lifted him to a sitting position. He saw the boats, converging on the island group of which his island was a part, and he knew that they must be using walkie-talkie radios to be summoning assistance that speedily.

All the islands were moving now, the smaller ones more swiftly, and the larger ones just inching their way along, moving almost imperceptibly.

The island he was on was of medium size compared to the others, perhaps two acres of bog. It was surrounded by a group of smaller islands, which had come on the wind and were passing it by. They would all continue on across the Flowage, not counting the ones which became hung up on reefs or other underwater obstructions, and then they would wait there for a shift in wind to float them back again.

The boats, he counted five, disgorged men first on one island and then another, and he could see the men comb through the low coverings of leather leaf.

By mid-afternoon, after having searched more than a dozen islands, the boats converged on the bog where he lay hidden. At once he began to slither on his belly across the island to the shore farthest from the one on which they had aimed their boats. He didn't have to look up now. The snarl of motors grew louder and louder, and then he felt the island shiver as one boat after another rammed full speed into it to slide their aluminum and plastic bows high.

The snarl of the last motor was silenced, and he could hear voices. He crawled all the way to a far shore, lay right at the water's edge, and waited.

"Spread out now," he heard one of the men shout, "and if he pulls a gun, let him have it."

There was no more talking after that, but he could feel their progress as the island vegetation shivered and shook under the impact of so many boots.

Finally Charley couldn't resist raising his head. He ducked back down instantly. Men were close. One of them said, "I think we've drawn another blank."

"Go all the way," someone instructed, "all the way."

Charley rolled like an otter, and slid silently into the water. Instead of swimming for it and inviting a hail of shot, he pulled himself close to the bog so his head was beneath an overhang of leather leaf and cattails.

One man came within a few feet of where he was hiding, and looking up through the vegetation Charley could see the glint of the sun on a shotgun, could see even that his eyes were blue.

Once it seemed the man was looking directly at him. Charley held his breath. The man squinted as though trying to focus his eyes. Charley was certain he had been discovered when the man turned and started away. Charley had to swallow a sigh of relief lest the man hear it and turn back.

Judging by the sounds, Charley guessed his

pursuers were withdrawing. He permitted himself the sigh of relief which he had stifled, and even raised his head so the water could drain out of his ears, when abruptly there was a shout: "He's been here! He's been here! Here are his boots. In a paper bag."

The boots! He must have dropped them while crawling away. Now he gave up hope. They'd comb the island, pry under every leather-leaf bush, look into every cattail clump and beneath every stunted tamarack.

He lowered himself deeper into the water. He stretched his legs, angled his body so it drifted to the surface beneath the island with only his nose and eyes visible. There he clung then, on his back, his hands locked into the bog's root system, like a bug beneath a leaf.

The fragile island shivered and shook and the men crossed and recrossed it. A half-dozen times posse members came so close he could see the frayed ends of boot laces or the stitching in the cloth of their pants.

He was just beginning to think that his presence would be overlooked, when a spider dangling on its gossamer web lowered itself to the tip of his nose. He curled his lower lip up, and tried to direct a blast of air toward his nose to dislodge the insect. His eyes crossed as he looked down. The spider was looking right back at him. Perched there on its eight hairy and bowed legs, the eyes were unmoving pinpricks set right into the plump body, and the proximity of the little beast endowed it, in his eyes, with gigantic proportions. Taking a deep breath, he submerged, and then when he was under let go the roots with one hand, and rubbed the place where the spider had been perched.

When he could no longer hold his breath, he let his face slowly rise until, like the head of a cautious turtle, his nose broke the surface. He wanted to gulp for air. Instead he controlled his breathing and it took a full minute to replenish his blood with enough oxygen so that he could once more think coherently.

Then he saw the spider sitting on a waxen green leaf, studying it seemed, this strange piece of flotsam which apparently was not able to bear even the feathery weight of its body. Its memory must have been a thing of only seconds, because once again it began lowering itself straight for his nose.

Charley watched with horror as the thin strand of spider silk came smoothly from the insect's abdomen, and then, just before it was about to alight, he slipped back beneath the surface.

He counted to fifty, and then slowly emerged. The spider was nowhere in sight, but inches from his nose was the heel of a leather boot.

His need for air was overpowering. There was a roaring in his head, and he could feel his heart thump in his chest. Nevertheless he contrived to take needed oxygen in thin wisps through constricted nostrils. Little by little, like drops of life being rationed to a sick man through an intravenous needle in his veins, Charley sucked air slowly, silently until his blurred vision cleared, until his head stopped throbbing and his frantic heart thumped with a more regular beat.

Above him the heel lifted, settled back, lifted again, and then was gone. Charley took a deep, anxious breath and expelled the air in a long sigh. Then, as if to store oxygen, he gulped air again and again, and his body fell and lifted a little with each breath so that tiny ripples ran out and away in concentric circles as it does when a muskrat busily chews on some floating green.

He heard the motors roar then, and knew they were leaving. Then, just as he thought the danger had passed, the boats came skimming around the island in single file so close that the fumes from their gas and oil mixtures was sharp in his nostrils, so close that the wake of each boat put wave after wave over his face, so close that their turbulence had him at last swallowing water and gasping for air.

When the last boat finally passed, he crawled out onto the island, and lying there, vomited. Water poured from his mouth and nose, and then, if any in the boats had bothered to look back, they would have seen him, half-drowned, sprawled on the leather leaf too sick to help himself.

He didn't move again until after the motors had been silenced, and he knew the search was continuing on another island. Finally it was a mosquito, spearing into the tender lobe of an ear, that started him slithering back toward a small huddle of tamarack trees.

Among the trees he sat up. Gradually he relaxed. Twice more, while he sat there, the motors roared as the posse moved from island to island. For the time being he was safe.

12

That night he didn't wait for her signal, but tried his own version of the loon's cry. There was no answer. He waited. To the west lightning flashes were climbing to the crests of the black clouds fast bearing down on him.

If she didn't come before the storm broke, she'd never find him. It was difficult enough, he realized, to zero in on one island even in calm weather, when that island was but one of a cluster of islands.

He wailed again, and when there was no answer, he contemplated swimming to the nearest shore. But what would he do after landing? Most of the reservation homes were on the far side of the Flowage. In the dark it wasn't likely he'd be able to find his way out of the forest, and, even if he did, by what route would he come to the area where she'd likely be?

The air was becoming more oppressive. He could almost feel the weight of it bearing down on his body, on his mind. It was difficult to think, and he moved a hand across his forehead as though to brush the weight of the atmosphere from his brain.

Half the sky was now black with clouds. The other half was filled with stars, but one by one the stars were blinking out as the cloud cover climbed.

He called again, waited, and then called once more. There! He thought he had heard something. He leaned forward as though that might help, and then the wind, forerunner of the storm, abruptly began to build waves, bend the rushes, tear at the little tamaracks and to twirl the tough little leaves of the leather leaf.

The hot night became instantly cold. When he stood the wind whipped his wet clothes around his body, and he could feel his skin pimple.

Then suddenly it occurred to him that his island retreat was a precarious place to be. He knew that an abrupt weather change in October might be followed by freezing weather, even snow. There was nothing with which to build a shelter, and wet as he was, he realized he might not last long if the temperature stayed below freezing.

He began to walk to keep up the circulation in his arms and legs. The tough little branches of the leather leaf bruised his stockinged feet, and the sword-like blades of the rushes sometimes cut through to leave red welts around his ankles.

He came back to the western side of the island where he had landed that morning, and looking into the wind, listened. The waves were increasing in size, and soon they were washing over the fragile island shore until he stood ankle deep in water.

In desperation he tried the loon call again, straining his voice until he could feel the muscles in his neck and jaw tighten. Then he dropped to one knee, and peered out as though by mere force of his own mind he might make the girl materialize.

He didn't stay kneeling long. The height of the waves was steadily increasing. Quickly they put a foot or more of water over the island. Suddenly he felt a lurch, then a sickening lift, and he knew the island was moving again. Then another lurch, an abrupt halt that sent shivers through the mass of roots beneath his feet, and he knew the island had come up against still another obstruction.

He wondered if the storm might not tear the island apart, and if in the end, he would have to swim for it anyway. The rain came, slanting and sharp on the wind. He put his head down, closed his eyes. As he stood, facing the storm, he felt the waves breaking around his waist.

Feeling fear course through his body, he threw his head back and like a trapped animal, let out a wail that lifted even above the roaring wind. Instantly he heard a shout: "Charley! Charley! I'm coming!"

Then the bow of the canoe materialized not ten feet from where he stood. It lifted on a wave and the wind hurled it up onto the island within a few feet of the shivering fugitive.

The girl never left the canoe, but extended a paddle. He grabbed it and pulled himself along until he collapsed over the gunwale into the bottom of the boat. He lay briefly trying to catch his breath, and then Betty Sands was leaning over him.

"You'll have to help," she said, pushing a paddle into his hands. "With the extra weight we're beached on the island."

He got to his knees, watched her, and then braced the paddle tip against the bog and pushed. They moved six inches, waves sent water spraying above their heads, then pushed again. The canoe backed another six inches. Then a wave lifted it, and at once the girl dug a paddle into the water and swung the bow around.

"Paddle!" she shouted above the noise of the wind.

He leaned forward, dug the paddle into the water, and the craft lifted and crashed into the waves. He dug in again, and then, with her coordinating her stroke with his, they drove the canoe off the island.

"Keep paddling!" the girl shouted.

So he bent almost double, and putting all his strength against the wooden blade, felt it bend. He whipped the paddle out, dug in again, and the canoe moved straight into the wind.

"Stop!" He heard the girl shout, and he braced the paddle across the gunwales and leaned against it, breathing hard.

In the stern the girl dug her paddle in, swung

the bow of the canoe around, and then they were running like a bird over the waves, along the north side of the island.

"Just sit still!" the girl shouted, and then the clouds loosed a deluge. Water soon began to slosh along the bottom of the boat. The canoe became clumsy and wallowed in the troughs instead of rising with the wave crests.

He felt a hand on his shoulder. The girl was right behind him. "Take off your shirt," she ordered, "and use it as a sponge or we'll sink."

He got to his knees, pulled off his wet shirt, and after wringing it out over the side of the canoe began to sop up water.

"Faster!" the girl shouted. "Faster!"

But the rain poured in faster than he could sop it up. The canoe floundered, lifted only a little with the waves, and then lurching precariously wallowed helplessly from side to side in a deep trough.

"It's no use," the girl shouted. "Use your paddle."

He dropped the shirt, picked up the paddle and dug in, but already there was so much water in the canoe that it was awash, the waves breaking over it.

"We've got to get out!" She was beside him, talking into his ear. "Get out! Hang on! We'll let it fill up. We'll drift. Just hang on."

He started over the side, and the canoe began to tip. Then he could feel the girl balancing it, and he let himself down into the Flowage. He got an elbow hooked over the gunwale and hung on. When

71

he could look up, he saw the girl across from him, hanging to the canoe with her right arm and paddling with her left. By now the canoe was full of water.

They made slow progress because now there was no appreciable surface above the water for the wind to lever on. But the waves were moving them, and so Charley began to paddle with his free hand.

Quite suddenly, and without warning, they came to a jarring halt. Charley thought they had beached, and began pulling himself forward along the gunwale toward the bow. Then he heard the girl.

"It's an island. We've run aground on another island."

He looked over at her, and she was edging forward. He continued, then, to pull himself toward the bow. Opposite the bow thwart he felt his feet touch the island. He stood up. The water was knee deep. If the canoe had been empty it would have floated easily across.

"We'll push it across!"

Then each got a hold on the bow thwart, and digging into the springy footing of leather leaf, they began to drag the boat. They passed the tips of stunted tamarack sticking out of the water, went past fat, brown cattails being flailed by the wind, and then Charley stepped off and went over his head. He drank water on the way down, came up sputtering and made a grab for the bow.

Then once more the waves were pushing them through the darkness with the wind dashing sheets of water around their heads.

When they finally touched shore Charley

couldn't believe it. He dug his toes into the sand as though to reassure himself, and then looked over at Betty.

"This is it," she shouted. "Let's get it ashore."

The waves helped. Together they dragged the canoe high enough to tip out most of the water. "Up on the beach, all the way up on the beach," she said.

They pulled the canoe beyond the reach of the waves. "Now, over with it." The canoe went over easily, and then she took his hand and was dragging him beneath the overturned craft, out of the wind, beyond the reach of the punishing rain.

Beneath the canoe she pulled him close to her, and they shared the warmth of each other's body, and the rain beat out a wild tempo on the aluminum bottom, the wind roared, and the waves reached and reached as if after them still.

But, for the moment, they were safe.

13

The sun turned the beach sand to a honey gold, and a thin shaft of light angled beneath the canoe and fell across the boy's face. He awakened slowly, not sure where he was, and then he saw the face of the girl—peaceful in sleep, her head was pillowed against his shoulder.

Sun beating on the aluminum warmed their beach shelter, and the boy leaned back. He couldn't remember when he had felt so completely at peace. All the years during which he had struggled for identity, the bewilderment of being an alien child caught up in a white world melted from him.

The girl stirred. Slowly her eyes opened, and she looked into his face, moved a little closer, and then closed her eyes and sighed. Then suddenly, her head came up with a jerk. "The canoe," she said, "they'll see it on the beach. In the sun it'll shine a mile!"

Then she crawled out from under and was tipping the craft upright. Charley got up and brushed the sand from his clothing. "That can wait," she said impatiently. "We've got to hide the canoe. Get over on the other side. We'll drag it to the trees."

Together they dragged the boat up the sandy beach, through the brown and broken bracken, and where a white spruce spread a voluminous green skirt, she stopped and said, "We'll hide it under there."

When they had finished, she broke a branch from a small balsam, and went back to the beach, where she smoothed out the trail the canoe, and their feet, had left in the sand.

"We've got to get out of here," she said. "They'll know this is the only direction you could have come, that the storm would have forced you to this shore."

"Do you think they know that you are with me?" the boy asked.

"I don't think so. They think you are alone, so they may feel they'll not have too much trouble running you down."

Charley looked embarrassed. "I suppose they're right," he said.

"Not now they aren't," the girl said with a little laugh. "Come on. We'll show them a trick or two."

She glided away then with long strides that

took her effortlessly over deadfalls, through brambles which, though armed with tiny thorns, never left a mark on her. Charley, noisily bringing up the rear, wondered how she did it—graceful and swift crossing the land with the silence of a shadow.

The forest floor lifted almost precipitously away from the beach. While Charley panted from the climb, it did no more than heighten the color in Betty's cheeks. When they topped out they were among sugar maples, endless aisles of towering trees. She turned and moved along what apparently was a plateau, and then where the maples gave way to hemlock, she slowed her pace as if searching for something.

"There," she said, stopping beneath a crippled white pine whose tortured branches angled out through a break in the hemlocks.

"Let's go up," she said, jumping to get a hold on a low-growing branch. She pulled herself up then, from branch to branch, and he followed warily. Halfway up the tree she stopped and straddling a limb, made room for him. When he was beside her, she steadied him and said, "Look!"

Charley turned his head, and through the break in the trees saw the main body of the Flowage sparkling in the sun.

"See the boats?" she said.

"Where?" he asked.

She pointed.

Then he saw them, like tiny insects trailing long tails of white water in their wake—eight in all—heading straight for the beach they had just left.

"They'll find the canoe," she said. "It will take them a while, but they'll find it. Let's go."

He started down, and then for the first time realized that his feet were bleeding when he saw the stains on the tree limbs. She saw the blood too, and when they were back on the ground, she pointed and asked, "What happened to your boots?"

"I lost them on the island. They found them and carried them off."

"Well, we'll have to do something about that." She pulled the hem of her blouse from her jeans and tore off a wide swath which left her with a bare midriff. "Pull out your shirttail," she said. He did, and she tore it off halfway up his waist, so he too stood there naked around the middle.

"Sit down," she commanded. He sat, and then skillfully, as though all her life she'd been fashioning makeshift moccasins from shirt and blouse ends, she wrapped his feet, tying the cloth around each ankle.

He got up and walked a little, and turned to grin at her. She was grinning too. One foot was beige, the other bright red. "New style," she said, laughing.

"Yeah, the boys on Brady Street should see this. By tomorrow it would be the rage."

"Just be a little careful when you walk," she cautioned, "or you'll be barefoot again, and with feet as tender as yours, you'll be crawling on your hands and knees before this chase is ended."

She started off then, and coming to a game trail, she turned and asked, "Can you make out this trail?"

He looked. "No," he said. "No I can't."

She dropped to her knees, and he knelt beside her. "Just look ahead. It's a dim trail, but if you stay on it the going is easy. It's completely free of brush, of brambles. The deer have been using it for years. The trick is not to stray from it, so stay close behind me and it'll be easy as walking on a sidewalk."

At first he had difficulty in determining for himself the directions the trail took as it wound through the woods following, as the deer had done, the lines of least resistance. But gradually it became clear to him, and then he tapped her on the shoulder and said, "Let me see if I can lead for a while." She smiled and stepped aside, and he went ahead.

The word "trail" for Charley had always meant a well-defined path beaten into the earth, a passage where the grass had been walked to death. But along this trail there was only an imperceptible break in the brush among the low trees. At first he sometimes wandered off, and always they would immediately be bucking brush. Then she would show him the way back, and after about a mile, he followed, almost as if by some long dormant instinct now revived, the winding way through the forest.

When they came to a creek he stopped. There was no sign on the other bank, no break in the trees, nothing to indicate where the trail continued. He turned to the girl. She had been watching him, and now she smiled and, walking to the water's edge, beckoned.

"There," she pointed. And beneath the clear

water he could see a slight indentation in the creek bed, a continuation of the trail downstream.

"I'd never have guessed," he said.

"Stay in the underwater path. The deer have made it smooth with walking. There'll be no stones to bruise you."

Without mishap Charley led the way nearly two hundred feet, and then abruptly he was bruising his feet, his legs, against stones and small boulders. He turned to the girl, puzzled. She took a few steps backward and motioned him to do likewise. Then she pointed, and Charley saw where the trail had left the creek, turned off, and continued on among the trees.

"But we'll stay in the water," she said. "Just in case they brought the dogs." He turned to proceed on downstream.

Where a tiny feeder stream married its water to that of the creek, the girl turned off. The feeder creek was hardly an axe handle across, and as they walked it became narrower and narrower and finally disappeared among a welter of moss-covered rocks framed by tall ferns, still green in this cool place, still upright because here spring water, never varying a degree from forty-eight winter or summer, had held off the frost while the rest of the forest had turned brown.

"We'll stay here," she said, "until it gets dark."

Then for the first time he saw the entrance to the cave, an opening hardly high as a fawn, but when they crawled through it opened up into a wide, rocky room.

In the center of the cave, in the sandy floor, a single tiny spring bubbled and sent a pencil-thin stream of water coursing down a slender cut in the rock. Over the years the water had etched, first a path in the sand, and then into the bedrock below.

"What do you think of it?" the girl asked.

"I don't believe it," Charley said.

"When I was a little girl I played here."

"It's fabulous. Like a fairyland."

"And a good place to hide," the girl said.

It was cool in the cave. The boy stretched out, and the girl unwrapped the rags from his feet and soaked them in the cool spring water before wrapping them again.

"Many years ago our people used this cave," she said, reaching back for a handful of loose sand. "Look," she fingered the sand in the palm of her hand, "pottery shards, only little pieces left. The best pieces went to the Milwaukee Museum."

When it was obvious he couldn't distinguish the shards in the palm of her hand, she picked out a piece and handed it to him. The size of a fingernail, it was hard and smooth.

"What'll we do?" Charley finally asked.

"Wait until dark. Then travel. We have to get back to where we can get food. After that we'll play it by ear."

"You know you've become an accessory to what they claim has been a murder," he said.

"I know."

"Why are you doing it?"

"Someone has to, and anyway, aren't we all in this together?"

"But if you are caught you'll go to jail."

"I'll probably go to jail anyway."

"What makes you say that?" he asked.

"Well, we're going to blow the dam."

"Not you," he said, sitting up.

"All of us."

He looked into her eyes, and then his eyes fell and he couldn't help but notice the soft curve of her breasts beneath the red blouse. "You could get hurt," he said.

"I've been hurt. A hundred times. Once more won't matter."

"Tell me about it," he said.

"You know it as well as I do. All my life, it seems, except during the four years that I was away at school, I've been hungry."

"But at least you got four good years."

"They were terrible years," she said.

"How was it terrible?"

"I don't want to tell you."

"You mean the white boys."

She nodded.

"They called you a squaw?" he asked.

"No, the girls did that. The boys called me other things. To them, every Indian girl had a price."

"What did you do?"

"Stayed away from them, stayed to my room. Never associated with any of them except when I had to go to class."

"How'd you get there in the first place?"

"I went on an Indian scholarship. I had wanted to be a history teacher. But I began to change my mind when all I read about was the glory of the country's western expansion. Never about the seizure of Indian lands, about the murder, rape and torture of Indian women and children. . . ."

"Did you drop history?" he asked.

"No, I continued with it, but, you know, there was never anything about how the white men annihilated the Indian nations. Nothing about the broken promises, the plundering of the Indians, the massacres. If it hadn't been for books like *Bury My Heart at Wounded Knee,* most would never have known about all the atrocities, about the violence and greed of the white frontiersmen."

"You should have gone on to teach about it," the boy said.

The girl laughed. "I'd have been fired within a month. And anyway, I'd had my fill of whites. I wanted to get back to the reservation. Even if I have to starve, it is better than being treated like an outcast. At least here people respect me for being a human being."

Charley was silent. He picked up a handful of sand and rubbed it between the palms of his hands. "I know what you mean," he finally said. Then he told her about the men sorting the Indian bones. He told her how, when only in second grade, a teacher had put him in front of the class and said, "Now, Charley, do a war dance for us."

He told her how the world had cast him aside, how nicknames such as Galloping Cow, Sneaky Snake . . . though something to laugh about at first, had become terms of derision.

"I was never comfortable. Not anywhere," he said. "I always wanted to go back to the reservation, but my mother wouldn't let me. She said I'd deteriorate into a nothing if I went back."

"Well, she was right."

"But you came back. . . ."

"Yes . . ." Betty said thoughtfully.

"It makes sense," Charley said. "In Milwaukee, when I was in fifth grade, a girl invited me home for lunch. You know what her mother asked me? She wanted to know what I thought about scalping. Me, a ten-year-old kid."

Betty Sands laughed. "You should have asked her for a knife. Offered to give a scalping demonstration."

Charley smiled. "Trouble was," he continued, "up to then, I never thought of myself as an Indian. After that, that's all I was. Every place I went I thought people were staring at me, pointing me out as an Indian."

Betty nodded. "I know what you mean."

"One time in a bar I ordered a beer and the bartender refused to serve me," Charley continued. " 'I'm not letting any Indian have any firewater. I don't want my place wrecked by no rampaging savage.' I darn near clobbered the guy."

Charley paused. "Let's knock it off," he then said.

"Just one more question," Betty said. "How does your mother feel now?"

"She's dead."

"Oh, I'm sorry."

"Don't be. She's better off. She tried the white man's ways. They didn't work for her. She made me try them, too. . . ."

They were quiet. He lay back down again, and she lay beside him. "Try to sleep," she said softly. "It helps."

"I don't think I can."

"Try."

"That's all I've been doing is trying."

After a minute or two, he was asleep.

When he opened his eyes again he saw Betty coming through the ferns.

"Where were you?" he asked, wondering how long he had slept.

"I went to the supermarket."

"Supermarket?" He looked to see if she was teasing him.

"Look." She pointed to the cut in the rock where the water flowed. "Dried blackberries, the birds missed them." Even as he watched, the dry berries which she had put into the water were absorbing moisture and becoming plump.

"What are those?" He pointed to a handful of red, fruit-like spheres the size of small marbles.

"Rose hips. Wild rose hips."

"And those leaves and roots?"

"Solomon seal. And this," she went on, holding a handful of small tubers, "is a distant cousin of the black man's soul food, the southern yam. If you could speak Indian you'd call it *bi-ma-kurt-wa-bi-gan.* It's not as tasty as yams, but beggars can't be choosers."

"And the rose hips and the roots and leaves?"

"The rose hips are for eating. Very nutritious. Full of vitamins. As for the leaves and roots of the Solomon seal, I'm going to make a poultice for your feet. It will help."

Charley laughed. "What I could really go for is one good cup of coffee."

"And if we dared to light a fire," she said, laughing, "you'd have it, almost. I saw some dried chicory out there. We mix it with coffee all the time."

"I suppose if I asked for tea you'd find something for that too."

"I would." She nodded at some foliage nearby. "There's Indian pipe plants, and the Indian pipe makes tea. In fact many years ago Indian braves about to go into battle drank it to make them strong."

"That's what I need then," Charley said.

"No fire," she reminded him.

"Do you think," Charley asked, "if we had to we could live in the forest without food from the outside?"

"I'm sure we could. We might lose a little weight, but you saw the trout in the creek. We'd build a stone trap for them. Then there are snakes. They're delicious. With a wire snare we could get deer, rabbits and even partridge, you know, ruffed grouse."

"I don't believe it," he said, shaking his head in wonder.

"If you were a reservation Indian, instead of a Sidewalk Indian, you'd believe it. Half of what you ate would be coming from the forest."

She scooped some berries from the water and handed them dripping to him. He put them into his mouth.

"They're delicious! They're sweet."

"Try a rose hip."

"Not bad," he said nibbling on one.

"Want a yam?"

He tried one and grimaced.

"Terrible?" she asked.

"Terrible," he said.

"Well eat them anyway. Lots of starch. Turns to sugar. Lots of energy."

Then she divided the rest of what was left, and they both ate.

When they were through she mashed the roots and leaves of the Solomon seal and mixing them with water, applied poultices to his feet.

"What time is it?" he asked.

"About three hours before sundown."

"See any signs of the posse?"

"No, but I can hear the dogs."

"The dogs!" he sounded startled.

"They're a long way off. They'll never get here before dark. Relax."

He did, and in the quiet cave there was only the musical sound of flowing water.

They left the cave at sunset. Though the sky above
was still bright blue, it was almost dark down among
the trees. She led the way along a game trail.

"Stay close," she cautioned, "and try to walk
in my tracks. It'll be easier."

But it wasn't easy, and they hadn't gone more
than a half-mile and he was limping badly. His feet
were bleeding again and so she detoured him back to
the creek where he could cool them in the water.

"I don't suppose I could carry you?" she
asked.

Charley Nightwind felt the blood rush to his
face. "Carry me! Never!"

"But you're not going to make it on foot."

"How far to the road?" Charley asked.

"Maybe three miles, but I don't know if we

should follow a road. That's likely where they'll be watching and waiting."

The icy creek water numbed his feet and he felt better. "I think I can travel now," he said.

They started forward. The first hundred yards his feet were so numb he felt nothing. Then the pain came back, and though the night had turned cold, sweat dripped down from his forehead and stung his eyes.

She turned once to ask, "You all right?"

He nodded, and then for emphasis, said, "Sure, I'm okay."

But she slowed down anyway, and he hobbled along.

She stopped more often now.

"It won't work," she said, after a while. She sank to a sitting position. He was glad to slump down beside her. "We're not making more than a mile an hour," she said. "At that rate it will take us fifteen hours to make it. We'll be traveling long after it gets light, and that's too dangerous."

He rubbed his eyes. "You go ahead, I'll stay here until my feet are better. Then I'll be along."

She grew suddenly angry. "Are you crazy?" she asked. "If you don't starve, infection in those feet will kill you. We have to get back to where we can get help. Even if infection doesn't kill you, it wouldn't be long before those dogs catch up with you."

Charley started to protest again, but his voice trailed off because he didn't know what to say. In the silence a coyote howled. The little brush wolf's wail climbed the scales to a thin, high, piercing skein of sound, then broke off abruptly and was followed by a frenzy of coyote yapping.

"My gosh," Charley asked, "how many are there?"

"Just one," she said.

"It sounds like a dozen."

The girl laughed softly. "The Old Men used to say the coyote strung out a howl and then ran back to bite it to pieces."

"How far away is he?" the boy asked.

"Not far. From the sound, he's about at the cave we just left."

"Lucky we aren't in the cave. He'd have us trapped."

The girl laughed again. "Not likely. The last thing a coyote wants is a confrontation with man."

"Well they sound fierce."

"It's all bluff."

The coyote howled once more. Then the forest was quiet again.

"I'm going to get you out to the road," Betty said. "Then I'm going to hide you. Donny Strong has an old car. I'll hike on over to get it. We'll come back for you in the car."

"But won't the road be patrolled?"

"I suppose, but we'll have to risk it. It's either that or I take you back to the cave, and then tomorrow bring medication and food."

"But won't the dogs eventually find the cave?" the boy asked.

"That's the trouble. Chances are they will. So we've got to risk the road."

The moon had risen by the time they finally reached the road, nothing more than twin dust tracks on either side of some grass.

"Only a little way yet," the girl said. "There's a creek not far from here. I want to get you there."

But Charley could walk no farther. "I'll crawl," he said, half-delirious now.

"You can't crawl."

"What then?"

"Look, try to stand. Then get on my back. I can carry you that far."

"You can't! I won't!"

"Charley! Don't be a fool! They'll catch us both if we don't get off the road." She whipped the words at him, and he struggled to his feet.

She backed up against him then, and reaching over her shoulders took his wrists. "Push up!" she commanded. He did, and with a convulsive hoist, she had him on her back.

She half-staggered under the weight as she walked down the dusty tire trail. Twice she had to lower him, and hoist him back aboard. When they came to the creek which trickled through a small corrugated culvert, she said, "Now you can crawl. The brush is too thick for me to carry you."

So like a lumbering turtle, he inched his way upstream, and then when they were in an alder copse, she said, "This will have to do."

She unwrapped the bloody rags from his feet, and helped him to the creek bank. He dangled both legs over the edge of the bank, and as the water closed over his burning feet he said, "Oh Lord, but that feels good."

Betty's eyes grew moist and she choked back a sob. "Now you can rest," she said, "now you can sleep."

The icy water on his feet revived him, and he lifted his head. "How long are you going to be gone?" he asked.

"Well I should be able to make five miles an hour. That's three hours to get there if nothing happens. Then a half-hour to get back in the car. Better make it about four hours." She pointed through the trees at a place in the sky. "When the moon gets about to there we will be back."

"Be careful," he said, and he could feel her breath on his cheeks as she knelt over him, and suddenly he wished she would kiss him, and then she did, a tender, soft kiss on the forehead, and then, like a shadow moving in the moonlight, she was gone.

Charley struggled to stay awake but couldn't. He was asleep almost at once. In the sky the moon climbed higher and higher, and in the forest the shadows changed shape. A coyote couple, teaching three youngsters the ways of snowshoe hares, yelped instructions, but the boy never heard. He slept until a car door banged, and then he raised his head and almost shouted, except some long forgotten instinct came quickly out of a neglected past, to throttle the sound before it lifted from his throat.

He heard voices. Not hers. Not Donny Strong's. Strange voices.

"Fill the canteen," a voice said. Then he heard the rattle of metal against the rocks.

"Let's sleep," another voice said.

"Here?"

"Why not here?"

"But what if the sheriff comes along and finds us sleeping?"

"He's probably sleeping himself."

"I don't know."

"Well, I know. Give me a drink."

The car door slammed again. "Let's find a turn-off," a voice said. "If we sleep here someone's sure to find us."

The car engine started. Charley heard the gears mesh. He heard tires whisper in the sand. The sound of the engine diminished. They were gone.

Charley could not feel his feet. It was as though his legs had been cut off at the knees, at the point where they were immersed in the creek. Lying there among the alders, he felt detached, a spirit floating high above the earth. Free of pain for the first time in hours, intoxicated by the moonlight, he was in a state of euphoria. He was almost sad when another car door slammed and he heard Betty's voice. Almost sad, because he did not want to let go of this aura which had so calmed his spirit.

Suddenly Donny Strong had him by one arm and Betty had him by the other, and he was stomping from the forest on legs which seemed wooden, and not part of his body. By the time they got back to the car, the pain was there again, and then when he was in the back seat of the old Plymouth sedan, he could feel the hot spots on his cheeks getting hotter. Now too there were spasms of nausea which wanted to break loose and bend him double.

The girl was beside him, and Donny in the

front seat maneuvering the car backward and forward, backward and forward, a dozen times before he had it turned around.

They traveled without lights. Donny leaned up over the wheel with his head almost touching the windshield, as he strove to keep the tires in the twin ruts.

The girl pressed a venison sandwich into his hands. He took a bite, but couldn't swallow it. He had to spit it out the window.

"I can't eat. . . ." he said.

"When we get back we'll get you some warm soup. It will settle your stomach."

Betty took the uneaten sandwich and folded it in a piece of paper, "They've doubled the size of the posse," she said. "Milwaukee has sent up more men. And, by the way, the Old Woman, Morning Star, died. They took her to the Burial Ground last evening."

"Morning Star? Morning Star?" Charley reflected on the name. Where had he heard it? Where had he seen it. Of course, the Burial Ground. The little girl. "I saw a grave at the Burial Ground. It had the name Morning Star on it."

"That was her daughter," the girl said.

"Her daughter!" Charley couldn't believe it. "But the girl in the cemetery died in 1898. So how could the Old Woman be her mother?"

"She was," Betty said. "The daughter was six when she died. Donny thinks the Old Woman was one hundred and five years old."

"How were they related? Donny and the Old Woman?"

"They weren't," the girl said. "The Old Woman didn't have anybody. So the Strongs took her in. That's even before I was born, maybe twenty years ago."

The car was moving smoothly along the soft, sand ruts. Poplars, silvery in the moonlight, were grouped like ghostly armies right up to the edge of the road.

"Not far now," Donny said, and then as if his words had triggered it, car lights suddenly loomed ahead.

"Darn it! Hang on!" Donny swerved the car from the road. It bumped through the shallow ditch, clipped off three small poplar trees, and halted in the forest. Donny cut the engine.

The car came slowly down the road, beaming a spotlight on the trees. The beam came closer. "Put your heads down!" Donny whispered. They ducked. The beam passed by just short of the car, then was gone.

"That was too close," Donny said, starting up the car and backing out again.

"How'd you ever manage to get in here?" Betty asked.

"Credit it to the Great Spirit," Donny said, laughing.

The rest of the trip was uneventful, and at the Strong house, Donny and Betty helped Charley through the lean-to with its smell of hides, on into the kitchen-living room.

16

The kerosene lamp in Donny Strong's house burned late that night. Shadows moved erratically across the walls, the floor, the ceiling as Betty and Teersa kept hot milk poultices on Charley Nightwind's feet and fed him partridge broth.

After a while, Betty went home.

Donny and his wife slept in the loft. Charley lay awake, with his eyes closed, in the bed where the Old Woman had died. Suddenly he heard cars in the front yard just a few feet away.

Car doors slammed. Within seconds, there was the sound of boots on the steps and a loud banging at the door. Teersa came stumbling down the open stairway and grabbing the black shawl from the back of a chair, threw it to Charley and whispered, "Keep your head covered."

"Who is it?" she asked, talking through the door. "And what do you want?"

"It's Sheriff Bascom, and I want to come in."

"You can't. We're still sleeping, and the Old Woman is sick."

"The hell I can't!" the sheriff replied. He kicked the door open.

Teersa backed away, an arm cocked protectively above her head as if to ward off a blow.

"Where's Charley Nightwind?" the sheriff asked, entering with the warden and looking about the room.

"Charley Nightwind is dead," the woman said, giving the stock answer. "He's up in the Burial Ground." Teersa backed away from the sheriff until she was leaning against the table.

"You know darn well which Charley Nightwind I mean," he said, taking a step toward her, "and it isn't the one in the Burial Ground."

"Where's your husband?" the warden asked.

"Upstairs. Sleeping. Or he was sleeping until you broke the door in."

"Where's Betty Sands?" the sheriff asked abruptly.

Teersa shrugged. "How should I know? She doesn't live here."

The warden went to the stairs and started up. Donny Strong came to the head of the stairs in his suit of long, gray underwear and stood blocking the entrance.

"Out of my way," the warden said.

"You got a warrant?" Donny asked.

"Who needs a warrant?"

"You do."

"Well, I can darn well get one. You know how the law feels about harboring a fugitive."

"Who's harboring a fugitive?" Donny asked.

"Someone is. We found Betty Sands' canoe. We know she helped the kid. We know that last night you were in the area where the canoe was found with your car, we know . . ."

Donny cut him off. "I don't know where you found a canoe, but I go to lots of places on this reservation. After all, it is *our* reservation. Not yours!"

The sheriff joined the warden on the steps. "Get out of the way, Donny Strong, or we'll move right over you."

For a moment Donny made as if to leap on the men. Then he relaxed and backed away.

The warden went up into the room and dropped to his knees to look under the bed. "No one up there," he said, as he came down.

Beneath the blankets on the Old Woman's bed with the black shawl over his face, Charley Nightwind held his breath. The sheriff went to the foot of the bed and looked down at him.

"Someday," he said, "I'm going to jerk that shawl right off that Old Woman and make her look at me."

"Why should you want to do that?" Teersa asked. "It's her way of saying the white man is a disgrace to the human race. She intends to shame every white man by never looking at another or letting any white man look at her."

The sheriff growled. "You're all a bunch of lazy, good-for-nothing savages. If any of you had any guts you'd be out hunting jobs instead of hiding here on the reservation. It's you who are to blame for the predicament you are in."

Donny, now in his trousers, went to an old, rabbit-eared, double-barreled shotgun that hung on a peg in the wall. He took it down, put a thumb first to one and then the other of the high hammers, and cocked the gun.

The warden and the sheriff backed toward the door. "You're crazy, Donny Strong. You're crazy," the sheriff sputtered.

"Maybe," Donny said, lifting the gun's muzzle until it was pointed at the sheriff's middle. "But my being crazy isn't going to make any difference to you if I pull both triggers. Ever see a man hit with two barrels of buckshot at close range? When the man falls, he falls in two pieces."

The sheriff's face blanched. He backed out the door, half fell on the steps, and the warden hurried after him.

Teersa closed the door. "Donny, you made a mistake," she said. "But I don't blame you. I would have done it too."

Donny carefully let the two hammers fall gently back to the firing pins, then hung the gun back on the peg. "I suppose I did," he said, "but how much is a man supposed to take?"

Outside they could hear the cars start up. When the sound of the motors receded Charley removed the shawl from his face. "I've got to get out of here!" he said, rising up on an elbow.

"Where would you go?" Donny asked. "You're better off here than anywhere on the reservation," Donny continued, when Charley didn't answer. At least until someone discovers that the Old Woman is dead."

"Didn't you report her death?" Charley asked.

"What's to report? An old Indian died. They die every day. We can report next week, next month. They'll find out soon enough. Meanwhile we can draw some extra rations."

Teersa changed the subject. "How are your feet?" she asked.

"Better."

"Well I can tell you this much," she said, "even if you are better, you aren't in any shape to travel. Not for a week, anyway."

"But I can't stay in your house! Every minute I spend here puts you in greater danger. They'll make it miserable for you, for everybody on the reservation, until they catch me or until they can be convinced that I've left, gone north."

"They're going to make things miserable for all of us shortly anyway. After we blow the dam, there'll not be peace for a long, long time."

Charley sank back on the bed, let his head down on the pillow. He could hear a small wind sighing softly through the pines outside.

"When you going to blow the dam?" he asked.

"Soon," Donny said.

"How soon?"

"Maybe a week. We've still got some problems."

"Like what?"

"It doesn't matter," Donny said, avoiding the issue. "You've got enough troubles of your own."

Charley insisted. "What problems are holding you up?"

Donny sat down at the table. Teersa lit kindling in the stove. "Like placing the dynamite," Donny said. "The dam is eight-feet thick. None of us has ever blown anything except stumps. The dynamite has to be placed just right. If it isn't it will only make a loud noise."

Charley sat up again. "Maybe I can help."

"How?"

"I helped set charges for the Army Corps of Engineers when they demolished an old breakwater in the harbor. We blasted eight-foot-wide jetties without so much as making waves so a new shipping canal could be dug."

"You mean you're an engineer?"

Charley laughed. "Far from it," he said, "but I know how to put a charge of dynamite so it will blow in, up and under instead of blasting harmlessly into air."

"Charley, you got to be kidding," Donny said.

"But I'm not. I saw every charge placed. I listened. I learned. I know."

Teersa had taken the lid off the black stove, and was toasting bread on a stick over hot embers. "Let's eat," she said. "You can talk later." She took two pieces of toasted bread, spread them with jam then handed them to Charley on a tin plate. Then she fixed two pieces for Donny, and poured coffee for each of them.

Charley took a sip of the hot coffee. "If someone could make a sketch of the dam, just a rough sketch, I could study it," he said. "I'm sure I could do it."

"I'll have to talk to the others."

"You do that."

Donny brushed some crumbs from his lips, then wiped his fingers on his trousers.

"Maybe I can meet with them too, maybe we can all talk about it," Charley said.

"Too dangerous. We try never to be seen together. That's why we meet at night in the forest."

"How many people are involved?" Charley asked.

"Really, almost everyone on the reservation. Hundreds, I suppose. Except there are only six of us who know that we're going to use dynamite, and who will decide when it is to be done."

"When will you next see them?"

"We're meeting tonight."

"Well . . . tell them about me."

17

The day grew unseasonably warm. Flocks of migrating ducks, and scattered flocks of Canada, blue and snow geese rested on the Flowage back bays waiting for colder weather to nudge them into resuming their North Country exodus. Walleyed pike, which had come upon the reefs and into the shallow water along the shorelines, moved back out into deeper, cooler places.

And on the bed, stifling beneath the comforter, Charley Nightwind threw back the covering. Donny sat at a window watching the uncommon flow of traffic stir up dust from the roadway which went past the house.

"You've really got things churned up," he said.

"I feel bad about it," Charley said.

"Don't. Don't feel bad. It does me good to

look out there and see them running around like chickens with their heads cut off, while you lie there taking things easy."

"But I'll go crazy just doing nothing," the boy said.

"Well, it's better than running," Donny said. "And anyway, where would you run to? They've got more men out there than there are trees. Darn fools!"

There was a discreet knock at the back door. Charley pulled the quilt over himself and covered his head with the shawl.

"Who's there?" Donny asked.

"Me."

"Come in."

Betty came in, her hair in burnished plaits, her trim hips covered by a scarlet mini skirt, and only a halter covering the top half of her body.

"Wow!" Donny said. The girl blushed and looked down at the floor. "Where exactly are you going all dressed up?" he asked.

"Not exactly anywhere," Betty said.

"Then why the glad rags?"

"Maybe just to show this Sidewalk Indian here," she motioned toward Charley with a nod of her head, "that just because we live in the woods, doesn't mean that we go around in buckskins and with feathers in our hair."

They all laughed. "How are you?" the girl asked, looking directly at Charley.

"I'm fine," he said, "and thanks for dragging me out of the woods. It isn't every day that a guy gets dragged out of the woods by a girl."

"You'd better believe that," Betty said. Then she turned to Donny and asked, "What have you decided to do with him?"

"Nothing," Donny said. "Just let him lie there. It's the safest place."

"I believe it is at that. Every time someone comes in, all he has to do is cover his head."

"It's happened already," Donny said. Then he told her about the visit from the sheriff and the warden.

The girl laughed. "I'd give a lot to see the sheriff's face when he learns someday that he stood in the same room with Charley and never knew it."

"He'll find out soon enough," Donny said, a worried look coming over his face. "They're sure to hear eventually that the Old Woman is dead. Then the truth will dawn on them, and they'll come running."

"That might take a while," the girl said. "So far as they are concerned," she added thoughtfully, "we're just so many rabbits back of a big fence. One Indian more or less, or even fifty Indians more or less, isn't likely to be noticed."

"I hope so," Donny said.

"Meanwhile," Betty moved over to the bed, "how are the feet?"

"Better," Charley said, throwing back the blanket. Carefully she undid the rags in which they'd been bandaged, and then, turning each foot, examined it.

"They look good. They're healing," the girl said.

"It'll take a while," Donny said, and then

changing the subject, added, "You know they found your canoe."

"Oh, yes," the girl said, "I had visitors too this morning."

"And you know," Donny continued, "someone must have spotted my car on Circle Road."

"No, I didn't know that," the girl said.

"My guess," Donny explained, "is that they saw where I went off the road and clipped down those trees, and they assumed it was my car did it."

"Whatever. They can't prove anything," the girl said. "Not that Charley was in my canoe. Not that your car was on Circle Road, or that Charley was in it."

"No, they can't prove it, but they know it."

Donny got up from the chair, and going to the stove, lifted the lid, put a few splinters on the glowing embers then shoved the coffeepot over the flames.

When the coffee was steaming, Donny poured a cup for each. The girl took one to the bed, and Charley lifted to an elbow to drink it. After the first sip, he said, "I'll go nuts if I have to stay in bed. I feel so in the way, so useless." Donny, who had gone back to the window with his cup of coffee, turned.

"If it will make you happy," he said, "I'll draw you a rough sketch of the dam, and then you can study it."

Betty glanced at Donny. "A sketch of the dam?" she asked. "But why?" Donny told her about Charley's experience with dynamite.

"Do you think you ought to get involved?" she asked. "Don't you think you've got enough trouble already?"

"They can't hang me twice," Charley said.

"I don't know," the girl said, "but it's a dangerous thing. Whoever sets the charges will probably have to make the approach in the fast water of the river. There won't be a chance to get to the dam on land. They've got it too well guarded."

"So!" Charley said, rather abruptly.

"Well," and the girl permitted herself a low chuckle, "you aren't exactly what you might call a skilled boatman. You'd never get through that fast water and to the dam apron without help."

Charley glanced away. "I've never boated fast water, of course, but what makes you think I couldn't?"

"I'm sorry," Betty said. "I didn't mean it the way it sounds. But the way the water comes over the dam, even a good fast-water man is going to be in trouble, especially since it will be against the current all the way."

Donny stood up. "There's no point in even talking about that part of it at this stage of the game. There are other details which have to be ironed out before we decide how best to make our approach."

"Like what?" the boy asked.

"Well, for one thing, lots of people have built homes below the dam since it was put in fifty years ago. We'll have to get them all out of there, or they'll be swept away, drowned. . . ."

"See what I mean?" the girl said. "When that

dam goes, whoever sets off the charges will have to get out of there fast or Lord knows where he'll land with all that water coming through."

Charley sat up. "Maybe we, you that is, could come by land. If there was a diversionary maneuver it might draw the guards off."

The girl's eyes brightened. "It's something to think about."

They could hear Teersa in the yard now, and Betty went to a window to look out. She called to her, "Hi!" and Teersa, her mouth full of clothespins, waved.

"You know," Betty said suddenly, turning from the window to face the men, "it just could be that we could run a line down the river for the canoe to be pulled up through the fast water."

"Maybe," Donny said. "Maybe."

Abruptly then, through the window, came the sharp chirring of what sounded like a disturbed red squirrel. Before Charley could know it was not a squirrel, Betty had melted out the back door, and Donny had thrown the quilts over Charley and covered his head with the black shawl.

An instant later the front door burst open and a half-dozen men trooped in. "We've got a search warrant this time," Sheriff Bascom said.

"But you searched the place this morning," Donny contended.

"Not your root cellar," the sheriff said, "and don't tell me you don't have one."

"Of course I've got one."

"Well, do you want to show us where it is, or

do you want us to tear this room apart and find it for ourselves?"

"I'll show you."

Donny went to the middle of the room, pulled back the heavy, hand-hewn table, and kicking aside a small rug, revealed a trap door with a ring in it. "Help yourselves," he said.

Three of the six men were obviously Milwaukee police officers. One of them stepped forward. "It's empty, or he wouldn't be so willing to show us where it is," he said.

"Oh yeah," the sheriff said, "then you don't know Donny Strong. Likely that's exactly what he hopes we'll do—go away, not look."

"But, if he's down there," the Milwaukee man protested, "and he's got a gun, the first man sticks his head in that hole is going to get it shot off."

"We'll see," the sheriff said, dropping to his knees, grabbing the ring, and throwing open the door.

"Come on out," the sheriff shouted, "You don't have a chance."

Frightened as he was, Charley found this funny. He compressed his lips lest a snicker escape and betray him.

"Well go ahead, Sheriff," one of the men said, "stick your head down in that hole. Take a look."

"There's a better way than that," the sheriff said.

"Like what?" the man asked.

"Like smoking him out."

"With what?"

For an answer the sheriff went to the window and jerked down the curtains of blue-dyed cheese-cloth. He went to the water pail and wet one, then balled up the other, and taking out his cigarette lighter snapped a flame to it.

"The Old Woman," Donny shouted. "You can't! She's sick!"

"Drag her out of here then," the sheriff said, and with that he wrapped the wet curtain around the one which was burning and threw the home-made smoke bomb through the trap door. Then he pulled his gun from its holster, and stepping back, waited.

Smoke quickly filled the tiny root cellar and came billowing out into the room. The men began coughing, then choking. Beneath the shawl, Charley was suffocating.

Suddenly Donny launched himself at the sheriff, shouting, "Your search warrant doesn't say you can burn down my house," he said, carrying the lawman to the floor.

The sheriff's gun went clattering up against a wall. Three men jumped Donny to pull him off the sheriff. They got his arms, twisted them behind his back, and dragged the Indian across the room. The sheriff scrambled across the floor and retrieved his gun. Still sitting, he swung the revolver on Donny, and shouted, "I ought to kill you!"

A puff of smoke clouded the sheriff's vision, and tears streaked his cheeks. "Let's get out of here," someone shouted. The room was full of smoke and billowing out the opened windows. They re-

110

leased Donny, and the sheriff shouted, "He'll fry down there anyway. Come on." They fought each other, then, to be the first through the door and out into the fresh air.

When they were gone, Donny grabbed up the water bucket, leaned over the hole, and doused the flames. Then he stumbled to the bed, yanked back the covers, and grabbing the boy by an arm, said, "Hurry!"

Together they staggered out the back door, and sank to the earthen floor of the lean-to. There they sat, gulping for fresh air, and waiting for the forest breeze to clear the house of smoke.

That night, the house still smelled of smoke. On his way out Donny paused at the door. "Charley, I'll tell them," he said. "We'll see if we can work something out."

"Maybe I ought to go with you, and tell them myself," Charley said, sitting up in bed.

"No. Let your feet heal. You'll be needing them."

Teersa walked across the room and gently kissed her husband. "Be careful," she said. Donny went out, and she gently closed the door.

"How do you feel about this thing of the dam, Teersa?" Charley asked.

"It scares me," she said, sitting down at the table and resting her elbows on the rough planks. "Of course, I wish they wouldn't do it, but I'd never tell Donny that. Even if they blow the dam, chances are they'll just build another."

"But they've got to try. We've got to try," Charley said.

"I know," she said. "But I still can wish that it wasn't so. It seems to me we've always been trying, and they have crucified us for it ever since the day the first white man landed on our shores."

Charley had no answer for her. His mother too had argued against opposing the white man.

"Don't fight them," his mother had said. "When you can't beat them join them. The Bureau of Indian Affairs has 16,000 employees, one for every thirty-eight Indians, and you know who benefits. Only the employees. The Indians are as bad off as they were when they were driven from their lands, and herded onto reservations. No, Charles," she had said, "you can't beat them, so there's nothing to do but join them."

In the end it seemed she had been wrong, so long as she herself had been concerned, and Charley told Teersa what his mother had said, and how, in the end, her efforts at being a white Indian had failed.

"That's what I mean," Teersa said. "It's like living between two worlds. We can't live in the white man's world because he won't have us, and we can't live in the Indian's world because it disappeared along with the buffalo."

Charley sat up and dangled his feet over the side. "But how can you go on if you feel like that? How can you face each day, each week, each year . . . without hope?"

"You learn," the woman said. "You learn," she repeated.

Charley put a hand to his forehead and rubbed, as if the gesture would help untangle the conflicting thoughts in his head. When he looked up at Teersa again, he said, "Look at Betty Sands. How do you account for a girl like that? She has hope. Right now she's somewhere in the woods plotting with the men to blow the dam."

Teersa brushed a strand of hair away from her eyes. "Betty has ripped a page right out of the white man's book," she said. "In school she was taught that any person who wanted to could better himself if he tried. And that is generally true—except only rarely do Indians succeed. Even blacks have a better chance. They have numbers. What's more, this is not their land. They too are reluctant intruders. It is Indian land, and many blacks are willing to burn it to ashes if they have to, to get what they want. An Indian can't. He makes small wars. You and your Coast Guard station. Donny and his dam. Little wars. The Indian never will fight a big war. His efforts are fragmented. The Menominees want their paper mills. The Chippewas want their special fishing privileges. The Navajos want their special grazing privileges. We live in a hundred, two hundred reservations all across the country. Each one is after something else. There is no united effort. Like the Christians, we go to a dozen different churches."

Charley's eyes had widened with amazement. It suddenly occurred to him that he had been thinking like a white man. All along, without meaning to, he had been characterizing this woman as an ignorant squaw, a submissive wife.

Teersa must have seen or sensed his feelings, because she said, "I too was educated. I went to the same school that Betty went to. I used to feel the way she does. Then when I saw that militancy wasn't going to accomplish lasting results, I thought as your mother did. But it didn't work. So I came back here and married Donny, and now, if I am not content, at least I can live with my decision."

Charley watched her as she took the chimney from the kerosene lamp, turned up the wick, and scratching a match, lit it. "Does Donny know how you feel?" he asked.

"I hope not."

"But then, why are you telling me?"

"I'm not sure. Maybe because it makes me feel better to talk about it. Maybe because I still feel that you should try the white man's world. You as an individual might succeed. Some have, you know. There are doctors, lawyers, politicians, other professionals with Indian blood. I don't know if they are happy, but they've crossed over, just as your mother had hoped to. If you don't . . . well, there's always the reservation, and like I told you, that's a special kind of limbo."

Charley shook his head sadly. "So much of what you tell me is contradictory."

"Life is contradictory," the woman sighed.

"Since you feel so strongly about these things, why don't you try to stop Donny from dynamiting the dam?"

"Well," Teersa said, "it would be cruel to

115

stop him. Then, too, maybe he will succeed. The valley may be drained. The corn may be planted. The rice may be harvested. It could happen. Maybe he'd die before they put the dam back. He'd have died thinking his dream had come true. He then would have been a success. They'd put him in the Burial Ground, and they'd talk about him like they talk about your grandfather. No, I'd never try to stop him. Never!"

"But still you think I should somehow travel a different road. Try to adjust. Learn to be a good Sidewalk Indian."

"Well, that's up to you. But right at this moment, unless you give yourself up, they'll kill you."

"But if I do go back, then what? Jail! I'd rather die!"

"You'd get a trial. You might get off. You might even come away free, ready to start again."

"Start again at what?"

"That's a question only you can answer."

"I've looked for an answer. There isn't any."

"You're young. You don't know."

"But you just told me there is *no* place for an Indian!"

"I said," Teersa explained, "that there is no place for the Indian as a people. There are places for individuals."

"But how would I feel? Wouldn't I be betraying my own people?"

Teersa sighed. "Likely. At least you would feel as though you were. But really you wouldn't be

116

betraying your people. Not if you take the long-range view."

"And, what's the long-range view?"

"The long-range view is that someday all people of the world will be one."

Charley pursed his lips. "If you believe all this, why aren't *you* doing something about it? Why do you stay here like a squaw?"

Teersa turned a little red in the lamp light, but quickly composed herself. "I am like the Old Woman," she said. "I hide my head. But like the Old Woman who made her contribution for fifty years, so in a way am I. I support Donny. Don't think for a moment that the Old Woman's contribution wasn't understood. That she never looked on a white man in fifty years is known on most reservations. She made a mark."

Charley lay back on the bed. It had been a confusing evening for him. He couldn't help but feel that much of what the woman had said was contradictory, except that underneath it all there seemed to be a thread of truth.

"You ought to sleep," Teersa said. "I'm going to the loft."

"Sleep well," he said.

"I won't sleep, not until Donny comes in. But I go to bed anyway. You learn. You learn to eat when it is time, and you learn to go to bed when it is time. That way you move from one day to the next. And I'll tell you something else," she said, smiling now, "no matter how pessimistic I sound, there is a secret place in my heart where I hope Donny is right. I hope that the valley will turn into an Eden for all time, and that I and Donny, and all the Indians, will be happy in that paradise."

She blew out the lamp. Charley heard her feet on the stairs. In the quiet far, far away a great horned owl warned all small, furry creatures that the night was his, and that now he was about to come hunting them.

Up in the loft Teersa, lay listening for the sounds of
Donny's feet on the front steps. All night she had
waited, her body tense beneath the blanket, her
mind racing along a high, narrow cliff of fear.

It would have been easier, she thought, if the
rest of the world had waited with her. But the earth,
never caring, continued on course. . . . Two deer
mice searched for crumbs beneath her bed, and a
family of flying squirrels, their tiny nails clicking on
the roof, sailed back and forth between the trees and
their home between the walls.

Finally she lit a match and looked at the
clock. Three in the morning. The match went out
and her heartbeats, loud in her ears, caught up with
the clock and matched it tick for tick.

But Donny was coming home—running in

the forest, over creeks, over deadfalls, among the trees—his heart also pounding, his lungs burning, the muscles of his legs aching from the exertion.

By the time he reached the clearing in which his house stood, he was stumbling with fatigue. Teersa heard him pounding up the three steps, heard him hit the door with a shoulder, heard him catapult across the room and crash into the table.

Swift as the flying squirrels she was down the stairs. "My God, Donny, what is it?"

"Get Charley out of here. They're coming. They've found out about the Old Woman! They know she is dead!"

Charley, up on an elbow, did not grasp the significance of Donny's message until Teersa had him by an arm. "Hurry!" she said. "Hurry! They are coming!"

A light swung into the yard as Charley fastened the belt of his Levi's. "Go! Go! Take this!" She thrust the blanket into his arms, and on bandaged feet he ran out the back door, through the lean-to, and into the forest.

Beneath the arching boughs which screened out even what little light there was in the sky, Charley Nightwind ran into trees, stumbled over bushes, careened through bramble patches, until he was breathless on the beach.

There he stopped to listen. He heard no sounds of pursuit, so he walked in the cold water on the soft sand the length of the peninsula until he was once more beside the big, black rock. He slid down, his back braced, and fingered his feet. Even in the dim light he could see the blood stains spreading on the rag bandages.

Now what? he asked himself.

Almost as if in answer the wavelets made a whispering sound as they ran up the sandy shore and retreated, ebbed and flowed in an interminable sigh. He would swim out to the group of floating islands which showed dimly above the water. If only he had a raft. A log. . . . Yes, a log. In what movie? It didn't matter.

He got up, winced as his weight came down on the freshly wounded feet, and walked back among the trees. From time to time he paused to listen for sounds of pursuit. Nothing. Only the forest breathing gently in the little wind.

He found logs, but it would have taken a tractor to move them. He went back and got the blanket, spread it open on the ground, and began collecting sticks. He worked until he had a sizeable pile and then wrapped the blanket around them. One end he fastened with his belt, and for the other end he took off his shirt and tied it tightly.

He tried to lift the ungainly bundle, and then decided to drag it. In the water it floated well. He pushed it ahead until he was neck deep, and then threw himself across it and began paddling with his feet. The blanket raft moved awkwardly, but slowly and certainly out across the water.

Sidewalk Indian? Maybe, but this was some sort of triumph, he thought, as the cold water numbed the pain in his feet, and the islands loomed larger and larger.

Now he had to dynamite the dam. It would be his answer for them. Then, if he came away unscathed, he could always go north, slip across the border, pass himself along from one Indian community to another, until he came to whichever Cree village might find it a splendid joke to hide him from prying, prowling Mounties.

The blanket raft moved slowly but steadily. Instead of stopping at the first island, he swam on until he was lost among the community of islands which had been brought by a common wind to wait in a loosely knit group up against a reef, a hogsback which had once been a winding finger of high, rocky land thrusting across the shallow valley.

He chose a small island, one barely the cast of a stone across, and landed. Slithering up on the leather-leaf shore, he dragged his raft after him. Then he rested, and then the sharp cold of the October morning cut through his wet clothes and he shivered uncontrollably.

To the east light was lifting. It changed the sky above the forest to dove gray, and the still hidden sun sent out its quick riders of brightness to light the way. But Charley Nightwind was not impressed. His feet were throbbing, and the cold convulsed his wet body until his teeth rattled like seeds in a dry gourd.

His hands trembling, he undid the shirt and unfastened the belt from the blanket. Then he scattered the wood, and crawling he made his way to the center of the island where he wrapped the wet blanket around himself and curled up tightly for warmth.

Gradually the interval between shivers lengthened. But he was never comfortable until the sun was a couple of hours high into a new day.

As he had known they would, the dogs started up shortly after dawn. Now they were silent, so they must have come to the end of the peninsula. It would be a rerun, he decided. A rerun of the first day he had sought refuge on the floating islands. The boats would come, and then the guessing game would start, and if they guessed right, they might catch him. If they guessed wrong, they would search all the wrong islands and darkness would send them back to shore empty-handed.

Warmed now, he sat up to await the appearance of the boats which would come like so many fast, fat waterbugs to zoom down on the island flotilla. But the sun came to what he decided was ten o'clock in the sky, and there were no boats. It moved higher until it was at eleven o'clock, and then when it was centered to the south, marking noon, he heard the distant throb of a motor.

Kneeling he scanned the horizon. First it was hardly larger than a fly. Then it was large as a blackbird, an eagle . . . and then he could distinguish the flashing light given off by the whirling blade. They were going to scan the islands with a helicopter!

For a brief moment he panicked. He got to his feet, as if to run. But where? Which way would he run? How could he hide?

The helicopter nosed down, then came treetop high, swinging and switching, like a great dragonfly. Back and forth. Around and around. Low enough to pick up the glint of a dime, low enough to hover and pounce with the swift dip of a swallow.

Charley felt like drawing himself, head and all beneath the blanket, as if the very act of shutting out the sight of the gleaming machine would make it go away. But his fear was not so debilitating that he couldn't see the foolishness of such a move.

Still, he had to hide. But where? If he could only dig a hole, crawl right into the ground, disappear beneath the earth's surface like a gopher.

That was it! Beneath the island! He clawed at the roots. Tore at the mossy bog, pressed and pried until water seeped through. Bracing his lacerated feet into the narrow opening, he widened it. A pool of water appeared. He put his legs through the hole, lowered himself. His feet touched the reef the island was anchored on. Like a snake divesting itself of its skin, he wriggled, squirmed, widened the hole until he had sunk to his shoulders. Sitting on the reef then, he pulled the blanket into the water with him. Then he sank lower and lower until only his nose and eyes and the top of his head were above water. Carefully then, he brought his arms up, and began arranging the bushes over his head. Covered, his wait began.

For a while he could see nothing except the sky above, but he could hear the roar of the copter as its blade beat the air with clumsy, throbbing strokes. Finally it hovered into view, crossed and recrossed an island near his, and then abruptly its weighted and seemingly weary nose swung in his direction, back and forth, as if scenting, and then it crossed over and swung directly above him.

Charley could feel his heart, pressing against

124

his ribs, thumping. The craft hovered directly over-head, went away, came back, went away again, and came back again.

Perhaps, he thought, his black hair was visible through the leaves. Perhaps he had so disturbed the surface of the bog while making a trap door down into the water, that someone aboard the helicopter had noticed.

Well, he'd know soon enough. The whirly-bird was descending. The air turbulence brought tears to his eyes. The noise preempted his mind, drove out all thoughts. Even the island seemed to shift, to move beneath the powerful wind blasts that flattened the leather leaf.

Then abruptly the aircraft lifted, swung about, and proceeded to the next island. Charley Nightwind closed his eyes and felt two warm tears slip off his eyelids into the cold water.

20

It was a black night. Clouds had climbed the sky to hide the sunset. A wind came up and pulled at Charley's long, black hair, and whipped at the loose ends of the blanket beneath which he sat huddled. For an hour after dark, he had imitated, to the best of his ability, the cry of the loon. But there had been no answer.

In the wind the islands had set sail again, and now he had no idea in which portion of the Flowage they were floating. Without a moon or stars he had absolutely no notion of the passage of time, and after a while, mesmerized by the gently rocking motion of his great green raft, he slept fitfully, plagued by wild dreams.

At intervals he awakened to stare at the darkness which crowded around him with such a feeling of substance it seemed he was caught in a smother of black fog. Shivering, he pulled the blanket tighter around his shoulders.

And if he was perturbed at his own predicament, he was worried too for Donny and Teersa, because certainly now they would have been arrested as accessories to his crime, charged with giving refuge to a fugitive.

His island halted abruptly. The jolt tipped him over. It was anchored again. He could feel that. But how far had it drifted? A mile, maybe more from where it had set sail?

Well, he couldn't just sit there.

But to strike out now, never knowing how far from the mainland, never knowing on what shore he might land, seemed even more foolhardy than just waiting. At the first light of dawn, when the world was brighter but still not bright, and he might swim unobserved, he would make his move.

Decision made, he slept, and this time without ghosts to disturb his rest. And while he slept the wind died. And the clouds slid back down off the sky in time for the Morning Star to shine briefly. And the sun came to the edge of the horizon and set out on its daytime course across the southern sky.

When he awakened the sun was halfway high to noon. The Flowage was placid, coppery. Islands crowded around the one on which he sat like a community of fat whales at rest. He stood up, thought better of putting a silhouette above the flat terrain, and sank back to a sitting position, but not before he had seen the canoe.

Now he wouldn't dare try for shore. If they weren't watching from the hills around, whoever was in the canoe might see him. Where would he find the patience to wait out another long day?

Well, at least he was warm, and that was something. And though he felt no pangs of hunger, he did feel an emptiness, except he couldn't be sure if it was an emptiness of spirit or a physical emptiness which might have been filled with food.

Maybe this was the way Indian youths felt when they made their ceremonial retreats to fast in the forest, hoping for the visions which were a condition of the manhood.

He lifted his head high enough to see the canoe. There was no doubt but that it was coming straight for the islands. He crouched lower, waited.

There was only one person in the canoe. It had no motor. So either it was a fisherman, a trapper surveying winter's prospects—or maybe! . . . He was elated by the thought. Maybe it was Betty Sands!

But would she dare come so boldly in daylight? He lifted his head again. The canoe was drifting. The figure in it was casting. A fisherman for sure. He sank back down on the bog.

Then he had no sooner dropped back down when he heard the plaintive wail of a loon, low but piercingly clear. He restrained himself from getting up on his feet.

Then he answered her, best as he could, and within minutes the canoe was edging toward his island. Then he heard her voice, "Stay down! Stay down! Don't move at all!"

He felt the island quiver as the bow of her

canoe bumped it. "Stay right where you are," she said. Then, "Are you okay?"

"I'm okay," he answered.

"Well, I brought you some food. And I brought you a pair of sheep lined boots. And tonight I'll come back and take you off the island."

She cast then, fished a top water plug, "Just in case," she explained, "anybody among the hills is watching with binoculars." There was a pause. He heard the plug slap the water, heard the click of her reel as she retrieved it. He raised his head just enough so he could see her. Then she said, "Donny and Teersa are in jail. They've been watching my house. I had a hard time losing them. They are sure I've been helping you."

She cast again, and the water churned. Then a big fish vaulted into the air, and the rod bent and the reel sang a strident song as the muskellunge took line.

"It will make it look more real," Betty said, "if I can boat this fish."

But the muskie was not about to be hauled in. Instead it took line, and adroitly pressuring the fish with the tip of the springy rod, Betty got it back. In and out. Around and around. The water whipped to a froth. But then in the end the big fish turned on its side, flashed its white belly of surrender.

"He'll go twenty pounds," Betty said. "And I don't want him alive with me in this little canoe."

Raising the rod tip she slid the fish alongside. Then she reached down for a hardwood club with a knot in the end. Holding the inert fish so its broad head furnished a convenient target, she slacked off on the line, and struck sharply.

The fish's gill covers were extended. A shiver ran through the bright, green, metallic-looking scales. Then the muskie was dead.

The girl leaned over. Carefully she put her fingers beneath the gill covers, and then with a sweeping motion slid the fish over the gunwale and into the canoe.

"I hope that will convince them if they've got their binoculars on me," she said.

She began casting again, and while she cast, she talked. "I put a small package on the edge of the island. It's got the shoes and food. Don't go near it for at least two hours, just in case someone is watching. Then when you do go to get it, stay down on your stomach."

Instructions delivered, she reeled in the lure, picked up the paddle, and the canoe began to move swiftly between the islands with its bow pointed for the far shore.

21

She came shortly after dark that night. By then he had on the soft warm boots, and his stomach had been comfortably satisfied with the bread and meat she had brought.

There was an extra paddle in the canoe, and kneeling in the bow, he added his strength to hers. Though he had rarely paddled any kind of craft, he quickly found the rhythm, and she was moved to remark, "For a Sidewalk Indian you can sure handle that paddle!"

After they were free of the clustering islands, they redoubled their efforts, and the canoe shot through the water making a hissing sound as the knife-sharp bow cut the tiny waves. "We'll go back to the cave," she explained during a moment of rest. "Likely they won't think to go back there. Not for a while anyway."

When the bow grated on the sand, he jumped out and pulled the canoe so it was high on the beach. Then she handed him a bedroll consisting of a blanket in which his supplies had been wrapped.

"Enough for several days," she said, "in case I can't get back to you. What's more, now you'll have two blankets for the cold nights."

Quickly she led him up the incline through the forest, and when they intercepted the little creek, they walked parallel to it.

Inside the cave it was darker even than under the trees—dark and damp. "I think we can risk a small fire," she said. "The flames won't be visible from in here, and at night no one will see the smoke." She paused and then warned him: "Under no circumstances start a fire during the day. You do, and they'll be on you like flies on a drop of syrup."

She went out then, and when she came back she had an armful of wood. There was the sound of breaking sticks, and then a match snapped and flared, and he saw the long shadows of her black lashes on cheeks which were amber in the little flame.

The wood caught quickly, and the flames chased shadows from the corners of the cave, and the heat quickly gave them a dry, comfortable feeling. The smoke went straight up in the draft and disappeared through a long, narrow slit in the ceiling.

"A perfect draft," she said. "When we were kids we chipped out the chimney so we could enjoy a fire in here without being smothered by smoke."

Charley leaned back against the wall of the

cave, and she sat across the fire from him, her legs loosely crossed, her elbows resting on her thighs.

"Eat if you're hungry," she said.

He shook his head. "I can't. I keep thinking of Donny and Teersa. What will happen to them?"

"Perhaps nothing," the girl said. "They'll make a big to-do about the matter, and then my guess is they'll release them. The Indian temper, being what it is at the moment, is nothing to trifle with, and I'm sure they know it."

"Where's it all going to end?"

"I ask myself that often, and when it's all over we'll probably not have gained a thing. We will have, instead, probably only have hurt our cause."

"Maybe we're going at it the wrong way," Charley suggested.

Betty frowned. "But what's the alternative? I know it's wrong to dynamite the dam. I know it's wrong to take the law into our own hands, even if it is the white man's law. Violence is wrong, I know that. But what is left for us to do?"

Charley reached over and put a hand on her arm. For a while they just sat saying nothing. The little fire, the heat of it buried in a pine knot, crackled and the flames threw fingers of light and shadow across the cave walls.

Finally Charley spoke: "But they'll only rebuild the dam."

The girl looked thoughtful, and then said, "Likely they will, but there's a chance, just a chance, that they might not. They're activating the nuclear plants, and perhaps they'll decide this operation is not economical if the dam has to be rebuilt. Then just try to imagine how Spirit Valley will look when the bottoms are farmed again, and the river goes back into its old bed, and the rice begins to grow."

The girl took another pine knot and put it among the embers. Imprisoned sap in the knot caught fire quickly.

"But what about you?" the boy asked. "What if you are caught?"

The girl shrugged. "My life is no bed of roses. My mother is sick. My dad drinks too much. Things couldn't be too much worse."

"But wouldn't you someday like to leave the reservation? So how could you, if you had a criminal record? Where would you find work?"

"Well, I've thought of that. I've always thought I'd like to teach, and, of course, anyone who doesn't want to get off the reservation has got to be out of their mind. It's a prison. It's a place to die. It's no place to live."

"That's what is so difficult for me to see," the boy said. "I'm learning to like it here. I can't help but like it here. If you ever had to live in Milwaukee, in the ghetto . . . well. Just think about it. Here are trees. The air is pure. There is solitude. Not a rat race. No cars. Peace. Don't you appreciate these things?"

"On an empty stomach?" she asked.

He was silent. What could he say?

"Of course it is beautiful," Betty added in a subdued voice. "If the dam went, it would be a hundred times more beautiful. And then too there would be an abundance, not of money, but of food."

"But isn't there any work to be found here?"

"Sometimes there is pulp to be cut. But not often. A dozen, maybe fifteen men have traplines. But there's no room for more, not enough fur bearers for that many."

"But you get government assistance."

"Who wants charity? And then, it's only a pittance. And we have to beg for it. And honestly, after a while who can live by bread alone. When pride goes the soul withers, the spirit dies. Her eyes were luminous. Charley couldn't tell if they were shining with tears or firelight. "Look," she continued, "I don't want the life of a revolutionary. Indians don't make good revolutionaries. They're idealistic but they have difficulty organizing, and they have no stomach for brutality. I'm not asking for much. I only want enough to raise my children in dignity. As it is, it would be criminal to have children . . ." Her voice faltered.

"Let's eat," Charley said to change the subject.

"What would you like?"

Charley laughed. She smiled. And then he said, "Pheasant maybe? Under glass?"

Then it was the girl's turn to laugh. "Well, maybe not under glass, and maybe not pheasant, but let's see. Would you settle for speckled trout? Wrapped in bacon strips and broiled over the fire?"

"You got to be kidding," the boy said.

"I'm not."

"How?" he asked.

"The pack. I put some hooks and a line in it. Now's a good time to teach you how to use it. We'll call it the education of a Sidewalk Indian." She dug

135

around in the blanket roll and came up with a green fishline wrapped around a wood splinter. Into each end of the splinter were fastened a half-dozen small hooks. Unwrapping a loaf of bread, she tore off a small piece, moistened it at the spring, and then kneaded it into a dozen tiny bait balls, each hardly larger than a pea.

She crawled on her hands and knees through the low cave entrance as Charley followed. "Sit still," she said, when they were outside. "Wait until your eyes adjust to the darkness."

Gradually the shapes of bushes, trees and large rocks came into focus. Across the jumble of smaller stones, where the land began to drop down toward the Flowage, they could hear the murmur of the creek.

"Twenty feet downstream," she said, "there is a deep hole. It should have trout in it. Let's go."

He followed, stepping carefully among the rocks. In the boots the sore feet were healing. Now he felt no pain. At the creek Betty turned, followed to where a flat rock edged over the water like a little cliff, and here she sat and made room for him. "Here. Sit here," she said.

Then she unwound the line from the stick and baited the hook with a bread ball. She lowered the hook into the water and let the current carry it into the hole. The bait hadn't been in the water ten seconds when she said, "There's one!" Hand over hand she pulled in the line, and soon a trout was flopping between them on the rock. She deftly broke its neck, and asked, "Want to try it?"

He smiled and nodded.

She baited the hook for him, and handed him the line. He put the hook into the water, and when he felt the tug of the current he played out line through his fingers.

Suddenly he felt a tug, then a series of tugs, and he set the hook with a jerk. The trout leaped and he heard the splash. "Pull him in!" He retrieved line, and the fish came slithering out onto the rock.

"A beauty," she said, snapping its neck. "Not bad for a Sidewalk Indian. Want to try again?"

He baited his own hook this time. In quick succession he caught two more fish, and then she said, "Let's eat!"

In the cave again she gutted the fish and split them up the middle. "A mink will get them," she said, tossing the entrails at the cave entrance.

Then she brought a small piece of salt pork from the pack, slicing several pieces for each fish, pinned the pork around the fish with slivers of wood, and then skewered each on a stick and braced them with small stones for broiling.

The salt pork dripped fat into the fire, and little flames spit up from the embers, and the blue and orange sides of the fish turned brown. She turned the trout, toasted them on the other side, and then handed him a stick.

"Man! Man oh man!" he said, when the first sliver of red meat was touching his tongue. "What a feast!"

"It is," she agreed.

"I wish I could live to eat like this every day," he said.

"You'd soon get sick of fish."

"I doubt it. I'd like to go back a hundred years, two hundred years, and live off the land."

"You wouldn't like it," the girl said. "I know. We live off the land. It's no fun. Nobody lives long, not off venison and fish. Winters are tough. Everybody gets sick."

"I suppose you're right," the boy said, "but right now and for tonight I choose not to agree with you. For tonight I'm making believe this is our land, and for tonight I'm dreaming that these are the good old days."

She only smiled, and said, "Enjoy yourself."

They ate the fish, sucked on the bones, and once she touched his hand, but then the fire burned low, and she said she would have to go, that it was a long trip.

"I wish you could stay. All night."

She didn't answer. "Be careful now. Stay under cover. I'll try to get back tomorrow night," was all she said.

He followed her through the cave entrance, and then sitting where the ferns were still green in the spring water, he watched until her shadow blended with the trees and she was gone.

On the sand floor of the cave, warmed by two blankets, Charley lay a long time before falling asleep. From time to time he added wood to the fire, watching the shadows chase one another across the ceiling like stampeding buffalo. The image changed again, and he saw the girl's face, fluid in the dancing flames, a thing of warmth and kindness, looking lovingly down on him.

He fell asleep then, waking several times during the night to listen to the coyotes, and to hear the lonely wail of a loon—far off, mysterious, plaintive.

In the morning he went to wash in the creek, and then he took inventory of his supplies: a small compass, some rope, matches, salt, dried venison, two loaves of homemade bread, two cans of tomatoes, two cans of beans and—he couldn't believe it!—a tiny snapshot of Betty glued fast to a bit of white birch bark the size of a playing card.

He stared intently at the photo. The dark eyes seemed to stare back at him. Then he put a flat stone in a corner, and propped the picture up against it.

Feeling at home in the cave, he neatly arranged his supplies along one wall, and gathering up the blankets took them outside to air in the sun.

Then he took off his clothes, unwrapped the bandages from his feet, and going to the creek lay full length in the water. It was like being submerged in cracked ice, he thought, and he saw his dark skin begin to glow.

Back up out of the water, he stood in the sun, and felt such a surge of well-being as made him want to race ecstatically like a dog chasing sunspots through the forest.

When the sun had dried him he dressed. Then he went to the base of a giant white pine, shinnied up to the first high branch, and then pulled himself from one limb to the next until he was high in the air. Nowhere could he see a boat. He lowered himself carefully, and encased his feet in the soft, protective sheepskin of the boots she had given him.

And the good feeling stayed. He wondered if it was the gift of his ancestors, part of his being responding to the primitive forest? And how many generations would it take to breed this affinity, this appetite for the wild places out of the souls of all Indians? Or would it always be there? Would it be waiting for just such moments as this to surface and remind any Sidewalk Indian that his gods were among the trees, and that spirits lived in the sunbeams, the coyotes and even in the flames of a fire?

He took such a deep breath he thought he would burst the seams in his shirt. Man! It was good to be alive! To be reborn, he thought. To suddenly emerge from the stifling years of sooty window sills, of grimy rain running in hot concrete gutters, from the narrow alleys where the sun turned yellow trying to get to earth—reborn in this clear, clean, intoxicatingly beautiful land, in the land of his fathers.

The surge of feeling exhausted him, and he sank to the ground to sit cross-legged on the small stones in the tiny clearing. He let his muscles go loose, let his mind gather in wooly feelings of contentment. Through half-closed eyes he could see the forest as through a dim lens which made it a hazy place with the mystical atmosphere of an empty church.

The rapid beat of wings, almost thunderous in their nearness, broke his reverie. A ruffed grouse landed not twenty feet away, and proceeded to strut back and forth, the ruff around its neck distended, its crest high, its wings half dragging, its bright eyes appraising him.

The bird's feathers were the quiet cast of autumn colors. It was an impertinent bird strutting there, arrogant cock of this forest walk. Indian bird, Charley thought, wild and free and unafraid. Strut! Strut! Charley said to himself. He felt like getting up and strutting too, chest thrown out, knees carried high, head thrown back, nostrils flaring . . . strutting, strutting!

Charley got to his feet. The bird's ruff folded back flat to its neck, the head crest was sleeked back to disappear among the other head feathers. It crouched as though to spring into flight.

If I could only catch it, Charley thought. If I could catch it, beautiful as it is, and even one more so there would be two, and then when she came I would be ready to broil them on the fire for her. If I could catch two birds for broiling and we could sit by the fire, she would know about this Sidewalk Indian, about how he has the blood of chiefs in his veins.

At first the idea of catching the bird was only something to toy with. Then it became more real. Charley dropped to his knees. Slowly he began crawling forward. Inch by inch, over the hard stones, closer and closer. Fifteen feet. Ten. The bird crouched again as if to spring into flight. Fast as the head of a striking snake, Charley flicked out a hand to grab the bird. Even as he did so, so too did the bird, and with that characteristic drumming of wings which has earned it the name of Thunder Bird, the grouse rocketed away among the trees.

Charley sat back deflated. He knew at once that never in a hundred tries could a man spring quickly enough to catch a grouse.

Well, he could go fishing. They could eat trout. But what would trout prove? She had taught him how to catch fish. If he could get a grouse, even one, they could each have half, and they could sit by the fire in the seclusion of the cave, two people sharing.

He sat back, and thought. A snare! He had

seen boys snare pigeons in the park with nooses of string. But what did grouse eat? Would they come to a bait of bread?

He could try. So he got the fish line, made a noose, and stretched twenty feet of it to a comfortable sandy place at the edge of the rocks.

From the cave he brought a piece of bread. He broke and scattered it around the noose. Then he went to the sandy place, and with his back against a rock began his vigil.

No grouse came. Even had one known about the bread, it probably would have presented no temptation. They are a bird for the green things on the forest floor. But a whiskey jack did dart down. With a twist of its head, a flirt of its tail, it picked up a piece of bread and like a whisk of gray smoke disappeared among the green pines. Straight away, another whiskey jack, eyeing the boy suspiciously, dropped down for bread.

Then two chickadees, chattering like black-bonneted old ladies, examined the bait. Perhaps they thought the white bread crumbs were ant eggs. When they discovered it was only bread, they flew away.

But the whiskey jacks appreciated the bread, and by shuttling back and forth, it took them fifteen minutes to eat all the bait. Charley wondered whether to put out more bread. Before he could decide there was a flutter of wings and the grouse flew into the clearing. As the bird took a step, he sat erect slowly, and without taking his eyes from the grouse, felt along the ground until his fingers found the end of the string.

The grouse was strutting. Perhaps it was the same cock, stressing his territorial rights. Though Charley never knew it, grouse sometimes will challenge the rights of such living things as coyotes or even man when these creatures invade their territory.

But it was not necessary for Charley to understand, because now it was only necessary for the bird to step within the circle made by the noose.

A dozen times the grouse came within inches of stepping into the noose, and each time Charley tensed himself for the kill.

It was a whiskey jack alighting that brought the grouse off its strutting path. Turning and coming forward to challenge the whiskey jack, the grouse stepped into the noose. For a second Charley could not react. His arm wouldn't move. He was cramped from waiting and had lost his strength. So he threw his whole body back and the rope tightened around a leg. There was a flutter of wings, a roar, and the grouse was airborne. The fishing string slipped from Charley's hand as the bird flew away with it trailing.

Charley got up, stumbled in his stiffness, and hurried to where the grouse had disappeared around a low white pine. He went around the pine, searched the low branches for his string, searched the high branches for a glimpse of the bird.

Then he began circling methodically. Around and around, out and out, widening the circle. In the end the string found him. It touched and tickled his neck. Being green, even as the needles on the pines, he hadn't seen it.

Charley grabbed the string and began re-trieving it. The bird fought hard, flailing the air, grabbing with its beak, its long toes at the branches. But foot by foot he pulled the grouse down, and then in the manner of the boys and their pigeons in the park, he wrung the bird's neck.

When the bird was dead and there was a smear of blood on his shirt, he had time for remorse. What had been a beautiful vibrant creature now lay limp in his hand, its head hanging. His pity was overshadowed by the feeling which comes to every hunter who has bested his prey. He had won fairly. The hunter must win.

He started back. In the sandy place he began to pluck the bird. When the tender skin tore, he skinned the grouse instead and taking the knife split it down the middle. He threw the entrails away, and in a flash both whiskey jacks were down to accept.

He washed the bird in the creek, cut two green sticks to spit the halves on, and took his prize to the cave. He laid sticks for the fire, even though it was the middle of the afternoon and he couldn't light it until after dark.

Then he went fishing, and when he had two trout, he cleaned and spitted them. Then he was ready—they could feast. He wanted to see her face when she saw what he had done.

The day went slowly after that. It seemed sunset would never come. He walked the creek watching the bottom shadows as trout dived for the shelter of overhanging banks. Twice he climbed the pine to look out over the Flowage, but there were no boats. Finally dusk began gathering among the trees, and evening drew itself slowly upward until the sky was dark. Then Charley went into the cave.

He lit the fire and sat back. He sat where he could see the light of the fire on her face when she came in. He wanted to see the eyes light up, wanted to see her lips part in a smile and hear her say, "Oh, Charley!"

But the girl never came.

23

Charley slept poorly that night. Betty came and went in his dreams, and each time he tried to touch her, she faded like mist melting under a hot sun. In the morning he felt tired. He climbed the pine, perched on the thick limb where he could look out over the Flowage. There were no boats in sight, so he came down.

His first impulse was to leave the cave, find his way to Circle Road, and go looking for Betty. But it would have been a ridiculous and a dangerous move. But what else? Wait? How long?

At first he only sat in the sun, knees pulled up to his chin, like an injured animal seeking the healing rays of the sun. Inside the cave the preparations for the forestland feast, the twin halves of grouse and the two speckled trout were still spitted on their green sticks waiting for their turn over the fire. They would spoil. Then even if she came tonight, he would not be able to show her with a special dinner how he was gradually absorbing old Indian ways.

Perhaps there was some way to preserve them. She might come tonight. Probably she had been watched, and not wanting to give away his hiding place, she had stayed at home. But tonight they would likely relax their vigilance. Then she would come. He felt sure of it.

Meanwhile? Well, meanwhile he would have to call upon such patience as had made his ancestors the stoical people historians said they were. So he got up, crawled out of the cave, and began to excavate by setting aside the fist-sized stones which were a protection for the spreading waters from the spring.

When he reached sand, his rocky hole was eighteen inches deep. Still he dug until he had a deep, cool excavation through which spring water seeped. He lined the sandy hole with rocks, then put the fish and the twin halves of the bird into it.

He found sticks and broke them to fit, and when the hole was covered, laid on brown bracken fronds to help insulate his cold cache from the heat of the day.

Pleased with himself, he undressed and after examining the nearly healed cuts on his feet, stretched out full length in the cold creek. He scrubbed himself with sand until his skin glowed and he could feel the blood bring heat even to his fingers. Before dressing again, he found a pine cone and groomed his shoulder length black hair, and slicked down the half-inch of beard which had accumulated in a silken covering over his face.

He climbed the tree and was startled to see a small flotilla of a half-dozen aluminum boats bearing down on his shore. From his vantage point they looked like silvery water bugs, and the wake of each looked like white-trailing tails.

They were coming to check the cave. He was sure of it. Perhaps having searched every other likely hiding place, they had decided to see if he had returned to that place from which they'd once routed him. There was but one consolation, he could see no dogs in any of the boats. Thus alerted, he might be able to avoid them.

Sitting there, high in the pine, flight seemed most logical. Then it occurred to him that he might lose all contact with Betty if he deserted the cave. To flee aimlessly through the forest might in the end land him in more trouble than if he tried to outwit them.

No, somehow he would have to keep the cave as his headquarters, at least until she established him in some other hideout. There was a way. He had a chance. It would require such talents as he hoped he might have, such talents as he imagined most Indians retained—even Sidewalk Indians.

He began his descent. Like a clumsy porcupine, he lowered himself from limb to limb, clinging to the rough trunk, scratching his arms and legs, scratching his cheeks and his chest.

When his feet touched the carpet of pine needles on the ground he hurried to the cave.

Kneeling he gathered his meager supplies and, except for the knife, placed them on the blankets. Folding the blankets, he knotted them, and took them to the forest, where he buried them beneath a deadfall.

At the cave clearing, he cut a pine bough. Then, back in the cave, he buried the ashes from the fire, and brushed out the imprints he had left in the sand. At the cave entrance he paused and picking up several handfuls of small stones cast them carelessly back across the cave floor lest it appear too immaculately groomed.

Outside he obliterated all fresh tracks, leaving only such imprints as had been made by the dogs and the posse during that night when they had first discovered the cave.

It was a tedious job. Sweat glistened on his forehead, trickled into his beard. Finally he stepped back, surveyed the clearing, and was satisfied there was no trace of his presence. He turned away then, but not before his eyes had hesitated on the cold cache with its telltale fronds of dry bracken spread upon the roof of sticks. Quickly he went forward, dropped to his knees, and carefully, one by one, camouflaged the food cache with fist-sized stones.

Once more then, he stood erect to survey his work. Voices were ascending the incline through the ranks of trees. Swiftly he brushed out the last remaining footprints and hurried toward the sentinel pine. Again he began the laborious ascent. This time he went all the way up.

Among the boughs he settled himself on a limb, his body pressed to the tree trunk, to wait. He did not have to wait long before the first man, looking small from his eagle's perch, walked into the clearing, took off a wide-brimmed hat, and with the sleeve of his shirt wiped sweat from his face.

Then quickly, one after another, figures appeared below, until there were twelve men in all.

"Search the area," he heard a man say. "And you two," Charley saw the man point, "you search the cave."

The men dispersed, two crouching to enter the cave, while the others disappeared into the forest. Only the posse leader, the man who had given the orders, remained in the clearing. Methodically then, the man began to search the ground.

Several times the leader of the posse dropped to his knees. Twice he picked up broken sticks and examined them. Then he edged toward the cold cache, and Charley Nightwind held his breath, as if by only wishing it, he could steer the man in some other direction.

Several times it seemed the man was standing directly over the hole where the food was stored. But each time he moved away, so Charley knew that he had not stepped on the rocks held up by the fragile roof of sticks.

Gradually then the men began to reassemble. Some slouched to the ground, and stretching out on their backs looked straight up through the trees. Charley tried to melt right into the pine trunk, and he hoped that any eye straying across his hiding place might hurry along never noticing the darker place among the green pine needles.

Some of the men brought sandwiches from

their pockets and ate, kneeling afterward to gulp spring water like thirsty horses. Two came directly beneath the tree in which Charley was hiding, and they shared a sandwich, and then shared the contents of a small flask.

A red squirrel suddenly popped from a knot hole in the tree and went clicking up the trunk, scattering tiny fragments of bark on the men's heads. One of the men turned his head to look up. Charley saw his face distinctly, saw that his eyes were focused directly on the boughs in which he sat, and believed that at any moment the man might sound an alarm.

"Squirrel," the man finally said, averting his eyes.

"Damn things," the other said.

Now the men of the posse were passing a quart bottle. The two men below got up and joined the others in the clearing. One of these took the last swig, tilting the bottle high, to empty it. He threw it among the now broken ferns and it glistened there.

The leader of the posse got up from where he'd been sitting with his back against the cave entrance. "What d'y'a think?" he asked one of the men.

"I don't think he's been here," a man volunteered.

A thrill of accomplishment ran through Charley's veins.

"But where then?" the leader asked.

"Who knows," the man said.

"Well, he's got to be somewhere," the leader said.

"Maybe he's left the reservation," someone said.

"I don't think so," the leader said. "We've got patrols on all the roads, in every village, at the state line and at the Canadian border. Someone would have seen him."

The man's description of the intensive effort that was being made to run him down, to capture him, gave Charley a sick feeling that went all through his body.

One of the men said, "We made one big mistake."

"What's that?" the leader asked.

"Jailing the girl."

The words jolted Charley. Involuntarily he moved and a pine cone went rattling down through the branches and landed on the ground. The men all looked up. Charley froze. "Damn squirrel," someone said. They all looked away. Charley felt free to breathe again.

"If we'd let her alone," the man continued, "she'd have led us right to him."

"Maybe you're right," the leader said. "When we get back I'll talk to the sheriff. Can't hold her much longer anyway. Then we'll put a tail on her."

"You'll never be able to tail that girl. She's a regular she-wolf. She runs at night. Ain't nobody going to stay on her tail," someone said.

"I'll admit she's good, but I'd sure like to try following—at night or anytime!"

"Maybe you'll get the chance," the leader said.

"I just as soon we don't find him. Not right away anyway," another man said.

The leader turned. "That's a hell of a thing to say."

"Well, why shouldn't I," the man went on. "I'm getting paid for walking through the woods. That's a lot easier than cutting pulp."

"Let's get out of here," someone said.

"Yeah, let's," the leader said, and he moved off, disappeared among the trees, and the posse fell into single file behind him.

24

Charley stayed in the tree until he saw the men string out along the beach and get into the boats. Then he went down. He dug his supplies out from beneath the deadfall, and put them back into the cave.

He had made a mistake, he decided. He should have given himself up. Then they would release Betty, the lawmen would leave the reservation and Donny Strong would be able to get on with this thing of the dam. He would light a fire, they would see smoke and come back. It would save him a fifteen-mile hike through country he hardly knew. They would take him back by boat, and then by car to the jail at Sayward, and eventually to Milwaukee to stand trial.

What else? He had only brought trouble to the reservation.

Yesterday was already only a dream: The grouse. A thing of such pride. What did it really matter? The surge of joy, the singing thing of happiness. Where was it now?

Now was the time to give himself up. Take his troubles back to Milwaukee where they would no longer plague the girl, Donny and Teersa Strong— free all the reservation Indians from suspicion and persecution. He had had no right in the first place to come with his troubles to this troubled place.

He gathered wood, dead sticks to start the fire, green limbs to turn the flames into thick smoke. Outside the cave he cleared a place of rocks, laid the wood in a cross hatching of sticks as he had seen Betty do. Then between his palms he made a ball of dry, brown bracken and put it beneath the pyre.

The flames came cautiously at first as if to taste the wood with little tongues to see if it was good. Finding the dry pine to its liking, the flames quickly united into a wash of leaping fire. He added the green branches of a maple, and then the thick smoke went straight up through the trees growing taller and taller like a column of white marble.

Now that it was done he was sad. Never again would he be able to climb the hill to the Burial Ground and look down on moonlit waters. Behind the bars at Waupun there would be no crickets measuring the temperature, nor any coyotes electrifying the night with lightning thrusts of sound. There would be no Betty Sands, not in that grim world of men.

Charley shook himself, added dry pine sticks, and when they were flaming, put on more green maple. Above the trees the column of smoke had flattened, spread a canopy, a white umbrella to mark this place where he was waiting.

They could not help but know now, he thought, looking up. And he wondered how they would come. Whether they would sneak quietly from tree to tree, or encircling him, come with a rush to throw themselves across the clearing and pin him down for roping.

It didn't matter. Already he was preparing, calling in all such feelings as might betray him. He would put them, his feelings, into storage, maybe forever. He would hide them, show not one tear, nor permit the heat of anger to strike any color to his cheeks. No remorse. Then they would know about a stoical Indian, and it would be his small revenge to steal from them such a measure of triumph as tears or tantrums might bring to their victory.

Getting up, he went to the spring and knelt for a drink. Then he sat beside the water and wondered at the stillness, not thinking that the smoke had frightened the chickadees from the pine, the woodpecker from its dead and hollow drumming tree, and the bluejay which had been chortling at the chirring red squirrel—everything had fled as from a forest fire.

It shouldn't take them long, he thought. Unless they made some other forays in other places thinking his smoke a trick. Devious minds, he had once heard, made snakey trails even along the dust of straight roads.

Well, eventually they would come, and he would be waiting. Perhaps, as a last sort of little triumph, he could watch them close in, then rush the smoke, only to discover that it was unattended. He pictured the consternation on their faces when they came to the cave and found it deserted. When they were ready to retreat, he could call down, like a voice from the sky, and say, "Why don't you look up here?"

He got up and crossing the stones walked to the tree. At the base of the pine, he looked up. It was a long, hard climb to the big clustering of branches which had only a short time before screened him from the eyes of his pursuers. He put a hand to the rough bark. Maybe it was a childish thing to do. Then, perhaps if he did shout, one or another of the more impulsive ones might shoot, and though the thought of a bullet did not bother him, the thought of falling all that great distance did frighten him.

He turned away from the pine and went back to the fire. Above the trees the smoke had formed a wide cloud, and the noontime sun shone through dimly, like a bright bulb screened by a curtain of gauze.

He might as well try to eat, he thought. He started for the cave and then stopped. What was that? He waited . . . listening. Perhaps an animal, a bird. He ducked into the cave and came back out with a can of beans. As he was about to drive a knife into the tin he heard something again. A branch breaking? A limb snapping back? The slap of a bramble against a leather boot?

He felt the urge to run. Only to sit in this

clearing waiting was an ordeal. Every age-old instinct which had made him and his ancestors
survivors demanded that he now fade back into the
brush, like mist vanished in the forest.

He put down the can of beans, took a hold on
the bone handle of the knife, and waited. No sound
now. He leaned forward, strained hard against the
forest silence as though by willing it he might hear
and translate sounds and movement beyond the
circle of his senses.

But he could hear nothing. No bird or even
insect, but only the sound of the fire, dying now as
the coals turned to embers. There was not enough
heat anymore to make the sap sing in the green
branches.

The sharp knife went easily through the can
cover. He sawed a jagged-edged angle in the metal
and bent the flap back uncovering the beans,
rich-red in their tomato sauce. He tilted the can, slid
the knife in among the beans, and balancing the
blade carefully put the dull edge to his lips and
sucked the food into his mouth.

He was surprised at how good it tasted. The
taste of food was good and he eagerly ate again.

He savored the beans, carefully licking the
tomato sauce from the shiny, sharp knife after each
mouthful. Staff of life, he thought. Beans—not
wheat—the staff of life. Beans and corn. How could
they taste so good?

He had almost finished the beans when there
was a sudden crackling of brush. There was no
mistaking the sound this time. Someone was ap-

proaching, so he set the can aside, gripped the knife handle harder, lifted from a sitting position to a crouch.

The defense posture was a purely instinctive move. Hadn't he resolved to surrender? He did not mean to fight, yet here he was ready to do just that. He had built the smoke only so he could give himself up, but now he was crouching like an animal at bay ready to lash out when the attack came.

His eyes narrowed. His nostrils flared. The short hairs along the nape of his neck bristled. Color left his face as blood rushed inward away from whatever wounds he might receive.

In an instant he had become a cornered animal. Muscles in his legs and arms and even across his belly drew up tight and hard. His mind became a thing of narrow purpose shutting out the sunshine, the trees, the beans, the ferns around him . . . poised—his body ready for combat.

The bushes at the edge of the clearing trembled, parted, and a man came hurtling into the rocky arena. Charley Nightwind lifted to meet the assault. The knife came back to give power to the thrust. The left hand was held wide to provide balance. The head was lowered . . .

"Charley! Charley! It's me!"

For a moment the boy maintained his combative posture. Then his defenses melted as his brain signalled all his other parts that here was a friend, not a foe.

Donny crossed the clearing and kicked the fire sending embers sizzling into the spring. "What the hell are you doing?" he asked. "Are you crazy?

You've got every lawman on the reservation zeroing in on you!"

Charley sank back to a sitting position on the stones. He was deflated, spent. The adrenalin had brought him to knife blade sharpness. Now it was gone. The knife dropped from his fingers and made a sharp sound when it hit the rocks. He took a deep breath, and relaxed.

"We've got to get out of here," Donny said, ducking into the cave and coming out with the two blankets. "No time for anything else," he said, grabbing Charley by the arm and jerking him to a standing position. "Come on! They were breathing down my back."

Charley let himself be dragged from the clearing. Then as though remembering something, he said, "The knife. I've got to have the knife."

"To hell with the knife," Donny said. "Just get your legs working, because believe you me, we're going to have to do some traveling!"

It was a branch, rather than Donny's prodding, which brought Charley to his senses. The branch, bent by Donny in passing, came whipping back to hit Charley on the bridge of the nose, a sharp, stinging blow that just for an instant drove everything else out of his mind. Then when the first sharp pain subsided, Charley's mind began to grasp the meaning of the sudden turn of events, and before they'd gone a hundred yards, Donny dropped his arms, and he fell in behind, loping along easily among the trees, around the deadfalls, over the logs, beneath the reaching branches, until they came upon a game trail.

"Now we'll give them a run for their money," Donny said, bending forward and settling into a rhythmical trot which was soon putting miles between them and the posse which had swept in from all directions to converge where the still-smoldering sticks were putting up streamers of smoke.

25

The game trail on which they were fleeing circled the sides of the many little forested hills, and then suddenly began to drop, down from the highland. Twice they startled deer. Both times the animals stood eyeing them before fleeing on ahead.

"We'll be there soon now," Donny said.

Charley was breathing too hard to ask just where it was they were going. Never before had his body been so taxed. Donny's pace was a lung-bursting, heart-rending effort, and Charley's throat became raw from just breathing.

On the banks of a creek Donny turned to Charley. "We'll stay in the water now," he said, "just in case they bring dogs. Don't touch the banks or the bushes. Stay in the middle of the stream."

Donny started downstream. The water, knee-deep, was icy. It ran swiftly, leaving bubble trails where rocks split the current. The swift shadows of trout fled them. Warblers among the trees along the banks were bright jewels in colored flight. The creek ran through copses of birch, beneath green boughs of hemlock . . . down, down through alder tangles.

Then where a lone maple looped a sturdy limb out over the stream, Donny jumped and pulled himself dripping into the tree. Charley jumped too, but exhausted, he lost his grip on the limb and fell back into the water.

He got up dazed. Donny was grinning down at him. "Come on, Sidewalk Indian," he laughed, "try again."

Furious at his failure, Charley jumped and his arms encircled the limb. Donny made no offer to help. For an instant it seemed the boy might fall back into the creek. But then, getting a leg up and over the branch, he lifted himself and at last was sprawled gasping on the limb, his body begging for a rest, his lungs pressing hard for oxygen.

Donny waited, and then when Charley was breathing more easily, he asked, "Feel better?" Charley nodded. "Good. Now we'll crawl to the trunk of the tree, and then out on that big limb on the other side and drop to the ground."

Charley didn't have to be told that the maneuver was calculated to dumbfound the dogs, in the event the posse employed hounds. The point at which they would drop back to the ground was a good fifty feet from the creek bank. Dogs scouting the creek shores might go straight past and never know it was at this place they had left the water.

When they were back on the ground again,

Donny said, "We've outdistanced them now. It isn't likely they'll ever find us." He moved off then, and upon intersecting another game trail, followed it.

The trail went downhill. Lower and lower they descended until at last they were up against what looked like a solid bank of cedar trees. Donny parted the wall of cedars by moving some branches, and disappeared. Charley ducked in after him.

They were in a cedar swamp. Once past the fringe of border trees, the swamp floor opened up because no sunshine could come through to promote the growth of ground cover. Mostly there were ferns and bracken, pale grasses and lichens on the logs. Within minutes they were knee-deep again in water, and the only cedars which grew here were rooted in hummocks of soft ground which mounded at intervals above the morass.

Quickly as they had walked into the water, so suddenly the ground lifted and they were walking out of it. Then they were on dry land amidst a stand of poplar and birch.

Here Donny paused. "We're on an island. An island right in the middle of the swamp. Likely no dog'll ever track us through the swamp. Anyway, white men hate to come in here. Somehow it frightens them."

Charley could understand how a man might be frightened. While in the water beneath a solid ceiling of cedars, the gloom had been oppressive, almost eerie. Charlie had had the feeling that he had suddenly been separated from a world that included a sun, clouds and stars, and the alien world was one of only dark water and dark shadows.

Now Donny proceeded at a reasonable pace over a well-beaten path. Shortly the ground dipped a little, and then they were in a clearing, and Charley saw three lean-tos braced between trees.

"Our main camp," Donny explained. He swung his hand toward a tarpaulin. "Our dynamite. Enough to blow up a whole town."

Charley walked over and lifted a corner of the tarpaulin. Beneath he saw a box, and in black lettering: DYNAMITE.

"Hungry?" Donny asked. Charley nodded. "I'll fix something," Donny said, ducking into one of the lean-tos. From where he stood, Charley could see that the lean-to into which Donny had gone was stacked with canned goods, supplies. The other two lean-tos, obviously for sleeping, had bedrolls covered with sheer plastic to keep out the moisture.

When Donny came back out, he carried two cans and a loaf of bread. "White man's beef stew," he said, laughing.

He put the cans down, skirted the edge of the clearing to gather small dead poplar and birch branches, and then built a tiny, completely smoke-less fire. When the flames had subsided to embers he placed the two cans right among the hot coals.

"Store-bought bread," he laughed again, and opened the wrapper and then set the loaf on the ground.

In a little while, bare-handed, he flipped the two cans from the fire, and then thrust a knife into each so twin jets of steam hissed off into the air.

The odor was tantalizing. "Take one," Donny offered. Charley grabbed a can. It burned his hand.

166

He dropped it. "Hold them lightly," Donny cautioned. Then he took a can, put his knife into it, and sawed it open. He handed the knife to Charley. The boy held the can with his finger tips, inserted the blade, and sawed a hole in the top.

Donny took back the knife and whittled two sticks until they were white and flat. "Spoons," he said, handing one to Charley. They each took a piece of bread and ate.

When they had finished eating, Donny got a small trench shovel from the supply tent and buried the cans. Then he dug a small hole for the ashes. He put away the shovel and came to sit facing the boy.

"Back there," he indicated with a wave of his arm in the direction from which they had come, "you were going to give yourself up. Weren't you?"

Charley lowered his eyes. "Yes," he said.

"Why?"

"It wasn't fair, all the trouble I had brought. Then when I heard them say that Betty was in jail, I knew I had to get her out."

"She is out of jail," Donny said. Charley looked up in surprise. They held her for only a few hours," the man continued, "because they thought they might be able to get her to tell where you were hiding."

"I'm glad she's out," the boy said, and then explained, "but I've got to go. Either that or surrender. You've got enough trouble without me gumming up the works."

Donny laughed. "Don't feel sorry for us. We're used to it."

"Still, I've got to go," Charley said.

"But we need you. We're all set. Ready to dynamite the dam. All we need is someone to show us how to place the dynamite."

Charley's face brightened. Then just as quickly it clouded over again. "I'm not sure I could do it," he said.

"Not even if we furnish you with a drawing?"

Charley considered for a while. "Maybe," he said. "Maybe I could."

"You've got to," Donny said. "All the people are expecting you to. The word is around. They think you're an engineer, an expert dynamiter. . . ."

Charley interrupted, "But that's not true!"

"I know it isn't. But you know how a story grows in the telling. Already the evacuation has started. People living below the dam where the water will come, have started to get out."

"It'll be a dead giveaway," Charley said.

"No it won't," Donny assured him. "Everyone is too busy looking for you to consider what the rest of us are up to. And then, the movement out of the downstream valley is a very careful, a very cautious thing."

Charley shook his head. "I don't know. I don't know if I can do it. In the dark. It would be hard."

"But I'll be with you. I know every square foot of that dam. I can find my way around it blindfolded. I've fished a hundred times right below the spillway, because this is where all the fish congregate when they move upstream to spawn."

"What if I fail?"

168

"Nothing is lost."

"But you won't get another chance. They'll double, triple the guard."

"We'll get another chance. If not tomorrow, then next day. If not this year, then next year."

"You talk as if you've got forever."

"That's the point. We have." Donny nodded his head sharply, as though to give emphasis to his words. "We've waited this long—fifty years—another year, even another ten years will not be so long if in the end it happens."

"You got dynamite caps?" Charley asked.

"More than enough."

"How about fuse?"

"I'll bet we got a mile of the stuff."

"You know it will take more than one charge. Likely more than a half-dozen, maybe even a dozen. They should all go off together."

"Can you do it?"

"No. That would take an electrical hookup for instantaneous detonation of each charge. But maybe I could set the charges so one would detonate all the others, and then the effect would be the same."

"That's it then. You've got to do it."

"And afterward?" Charley hesitated, looked into the man's eyes.

"What do you mean, 'afterward'?"

"Never mind."

"No, tell me."

"Where will I go?"

Donny picked up a stick and fiddled with it. He turned the stick over and over with his fingers.

Then he jammed it into the ground. "You stay," he said. "We can't guarantee they won't catch you, but with every Indian on the reservation helping, we'll give them enough trouble so that in the end . . ."

"They won't," the boy cut in. "They won't stop looking."

Donny broke off the stick he had jammed into the ground. "You're right. They won't. They'll keep on looking. I'm sorry."

"Don't be. I'm the one who should be sorry. You've done enough, too much for me already. For a while it didn't seem to matter. I wanted to give myself up. Now I don't. . . ."

"Betty?" Donny asked.

Charley nodded.

"But you may get off. They just might discover that you didn't do it, find you not guilty. Then you could come back."

"It really doesn't matter," Charley said, holding up a hand as though to silence the man. "I'm sorry I even spoke about it."

"But it does matter. Lots of the people, especially the old folks, look on you as the man to rightfully be their chief."

Charley laughed. "That's a joke. That's real funny. A Sidewalk Indian from Milwaukee a chief. About the only thing I could qualify as chief of would be the high school Ping-Pong team."

"But the people need a tie with their past. You could be that link to the life their people once had. You are a descendant of chiefs. Your grandfather came from a long line of chiefs. You could carry on. It would give the people a sense of identity, of continuity. It would give them the feeling that in spite of everything they might survive as a people so long as the rule of chiefs is passed on down from one generation to the next."

Charley was smiling. "You're quite an orator. Maybe you should have been a politician."

Then Donny laughed too. "I suppose I do run off at the mouth, but I mean it. I know chiefs today have little or no power, but it would give the older people something to believe in, and it would give the youngsters someone to look up to."

"No way," Charley said. Then he repeated himself, "No way. I couldn't be a chief."

Donny threw up his hands. "I didn't think you would, but maybe if you lived with us for a while, learned our ways, you might change your mind."

Charley didn't answer. He merely shrugged.

"Then if you successfully dynamited the dam you'd be a hero. The people would have every reason, every right to make you a chief, and it would be wrong for you to turn them down."

"What good would a chief be behind bars in Waupun?"

"Many chiefs were held as hostages during the white man's invasion of the West. This made them no less important to the people."

Charley stood up. "Absolutely not!" he almost shouted. "First off, I don't qualify. Secondly, I don't believe in chiefs. I believe in democracy, a council of the people."

"Okay, okay. Just forget I mentioned it."

Charley sat back down. He looked earnestly at the older man. Then he said quietly, "I won't be a chief, Donny, but I will dynamite the dam."

Evening came swiftly to the clearing. Surrounded as it was by high, gnarled cedars, the small forest segment of poplar and birch which marked the small island was lost to the sun early in the afternoon.

Donny Strong was sleeping. Charley had tried to sleep, but tired as his body was, his mind raced ahead contemplating the dangers of days to come.

He supposed he should pray. But to whom? Implore the spirits of his ancestors which lived even in rocks? Or seek help from the white man's God, the one they claimed was the sole arbiter of man's destiny?

But why pray in the first place? If his conduct throughout all the years of his life hadn't been exemplary enough to merit the attention of the One God, or any of the Indian gods, then prayer was a bribe, and maybe to try to corrupt a god was the most vicious of all sins.

Throw them away, he thought. Throw away the thoughts of gods and God. Just sleep so tortured muscles might become soft under their sheaths of skin, soft for healing and growing strong again.

At last he slept. But just before he closed his eyes the setting sun found a slender break among the surrounding cedars and a shaft of light poured into the clearing and he lay for a few seconds in a blaze of brilliance. Then he couldn't help wondering, in spite of everything, if he hadn't been given a sign.

In the darkness which soon followed, he did not hear the men come out of the swamp to sit in the clearing. He never knew the girl was there, seated among the men, in a council of war.

A coyote had announced sunset with a quavering salute to evening, and then the minutes of the night had been ticked off by one shiny, black cricket which had found enough warmth for a celebration where the ashes of the fire had been buried.

The moon had risen by the time he awakened, and though the slanting rays never penetrated the clearing, the stars began to pale. Maybe the horned owls preferred help from the light of the moon, because at once three, then four let it be known, hooting boldly, that they now would patrol the forest aisles.

Charley shivered. He heard voices and turned his head. As he was about to get up and walk over to where the men were seated in a circle, he recognized Betty's voice. At once his heartbeat quickened.

So engrossed were the seven that at first they did not know that he was standing there. He took another step, and he must have come within the cricket's sphere, because suddenly the insect stopped chirping, and at once every head was turned in his direction.

"Charley," Donny called, "come on, we've been waiting for you to wake up."

Betty made room for him beside her. "Hi," she said. He felt blood rush to his face and was thankful the darkness hid his blush.

He sat, and he could smell her freshness, and then Donny was talking: "Everything is about ready. Tomorrow night or the next night. We've just been reviewing things."

At first Charley didn't grasp the significance of Donny's words. The girl's presence, the feel of her so close, the perfume of her hair . . . overwhelmed him.

It was only gradually that his mind began to focus on what was being said. Donny was asking, "Who checked out the people below the dam?"

"I did," Betty answered.

"How are they coming?" Donny asked.

"Most have already moved. The rest are moving tonight. I drove both roads, the High Road on the west and the Low Road on the east. I didn't miss a home. I talked to everyone, all those who still hadn't moved. They said they'd all be out by tomorrow night."

"Think anyone suspects anything yet?" asked Donny.

One of the men said, "They're too busy looking for your friend. They've not even noticed that the river valley has been evacuated."

Charley leaned forward. The one who had spoken was the eagle-beaked one. Charley remembered. He looked at the others. They were the same men he had met the night the girl took him from the floating island.

"Who checked the guards at the dam?" Donny asked.

One of the men raised a hand. "I did. They've reduced the guard from eight to two. I think the rest are combing the forest for Charley."

"Know who the two are?" Donny asked.

"Yeah. Night watchmen from the paper mill. Old Frazer and that one-legged fellow. I think his name is Rasmussen. Both must be in their seventies."

"They probably go to sleep by midnight," one of the men said.

"We can't count on that," Donny said.

"Well," the man with the eagle-beak said, "they'll never hear anything above the noise of the water."

"What time does the moon rise?" Donny asked.

"About eleven," Betty said.

"Which means that by eleven all the charges must have been placed," Charley offered.

"There's one thing you're forgetting."

"What's that, Turlene?" Donny asked.

"The weather. It is supposed to get cold, real

176

cold. There's a front moving in tomorrow. That dam will be sheathed in ice. Whoever sets the charges will have one hell of a time trying to get around if the whole thing is coated with ice."

"No chance," another man said. "It has to go below zero. It'll never drop that low before tomorrow night."

"I've seen it happen," Turlene said.

"If it does we'll just have to postpone the operation," Donny interjected. Then he continued: "Now for the important part. Who's got a sketch of the dam?"

"Wilbur drew it," the eagle-beaked one offered.

Wilbur was unrolling a three-foot square of heavy paper. He put stones and sticks on it to make it lay flat. Then Turlene shined the flashlight on the drawing.

The penciled lines seemed to leap into prominence. "It's a good drawing," Charley said at once. "And I can tell you one thing right off, if we can't get charges under that concrete apron we'll never budge that dam."

The concrete apron formed a spillway for the water, and it was the foundation on which the entire structure rested.

"If we can't get under here," Charley continued, "we aren't going to do much damage. And to get under here means drilling."

"Maybe not," Donny said.

"But how else?" Charley asked.

"I'll tell you. For fifty years now muskrats have been tunneling under that apron hoping to be able to drive holes up through the concrete to get burrows above the water level. Of course, they've never succeeded, but they keep trying, and as fast as the dam repair crew plugs the holes, they dig new ones."

"How far back are the holes likely to penetrate?" Charley asked.

Donny pursed his lips thoughtfully. "Some maybe twenty feet. Maybe even further."

"If that's true," Charley said, "and we can get charges under the apron, we should be able to break the dam up."

Then swiftly he indicated the places at which dynamite charges would be most effective. "Four beneath the apron," he said, "one each for the abutments. Four more right down into the water along the face, the Flowage side of the dam. I'm sure that will do it."

"That's a big order," the eagle-beaked one said.

"It'll take some doing," Charley said, "but if the charges are placed right, the ones under the apron should detonate the others. Then if we're lucky, the whole thing should cave right in on itself."

Charley was surprised at how confident he sounded. He didn't feel confident. He was frightened, and he wasn't at all sure that his plan would work. He only knew that the charges had to be placed so one blast would be working against another instead of breaking away harmlessly into air. He wondered if he had gone too far.

"Maybe I ought to spend a night looking the dam over," Charley said. Then he felt Betty's fingers close over his arm. He turned to look at her. She gave him just the suggestion of a smile. Then he quickly added, "But it shouldn't really be necessary. The drawing really tells me all I need to know," he concluded.

"Well, now that that's settled," Donny said, "let's figure how we're going to get out of there after the fuse has been lighted."

"In the first place, who's going in with the kid?" the eagle-beaked one asked.

"I am," Donny said. "No one else."

"Well," the eagle-beaked one acknowledged with a bow of his head, "then you better plan on getting out of the river right below the first rapids."

Turlene spoke up: "That's right. There's a good trail there up to the High Road. They carry boats down it to make river trips."

"How far from the dam?" Charley asked.

"Maybe three hundred yards," Donny said.

"Will a three-minute fuse get us out of there?" Charley asked.

"It'll be a close squeak."

"But a long fuse increases the danger of discovery, and lots of things can happen before a long fuse brings the fire to the dynamite. A ten-second fuse is better. Three minutes is really stretching it."

Donny lowered his head. "I think we can get out in three minutes," he said.

Charley felt Betty's fingers tighten on his arm. He looked at her, and this time she did not try to smile.

Quickly the plans were laid for diverting the

attention of the guards. Turlene said he would have a canoe hidden in the brush below the first rapids. Wilbur said he would be waiting in a truck on the High Road to get them out of the area ahead of the rush of water.

Then Charley turned to Betty. "Where will you be?"

"In jail," she said, laughing.

"In jail!"

"That's right," the eagle-beaked one said. "She's going to throw a rock through a jail window tomorrow afternoon. They'll jail her. Then in the evening every Indian on the reservation will be building protest bonfires in front of the jail. That'll keep most of the sheriff's men occupied while the dam is being dynamited."

It was a well-planned battle maneuver, Charley saw that now. It was no hastily concocted scheme, no protest of the moment as had been the Coast Guard melee in Milwaukee. And it might work. It might work if he placed the dynamite where it would fracture the dam so the force of the water could tear it apart.

27

Next afternoon Donny and Charley came to the crest of a high hill overlooking the Spirit River. An old burn which had cleared a wide swath of forest, gave them an unobstructed view of the valley below. The dam gleamed, an alien white barricade, in an endless reach of trees. Behind the dam, waters of the Flowage were blue as the little wild asters along the edge of the burn. Below the dam the Spirit River was a tortured, twisted skein, black in the quiet places, white where rapids frothed.

The pair stood for a moment looking around. Then they undid their pack straps and slipped the bundles of dynamite carefully to the ground. To the back of one pack was coiled yard after yard of rope, and to the back of the other was tied a collapsible trench shovel. Donny dropped to his knees beside the packs, lifted the binoculars which hung around his neck, and scanned the valley.

Last night, after the men had left and Donny had gone to a lean-to to sleep, Charley and Betty had walked to the edge of the island and there he had taken her into his arms. The sweetness of the interlude, their moment of love, had been like coming to the quiet eye of a hurricane and there, while wild winds played out their violent roles around them, they had found peace.

The feeling remained with the boy even after she had left, and it was with him all morning while they taped dynamite into explosive units of six sticks each. The soft sweetness of her touch still lingered even as they crouched on the summit looking down on the valley.

"Only two guards," Donny said, handing Charley the glasses.

At first, Charley couldn't find the men. Then they came into view. Both were in the shade of the catwalk, a slender bridge, stretching from abutment to abutment across the top of the dam. Both were smoking pipes, and their little lever action carbines were leaning against the rail.

Charley moved the binoculars, swept them to the left and downstream. "There's somebody on the bank," he said.

Donny took the glasses, focused, and then leaned forward to look. "It's Turlene," he said. "he's brought the canoe. I can see the alders where he's hidden it." He passed the glasses back but by the time Charley got them to his eyes, Turlene had vanished in the brush. Charley moved the glasses back to the dam, and bracing his elbows on his knees, sat studying the structure.

"Well?" Donny asked, "what do you think?"

"It's enormous," Charley said. "Much bigger than I thought. I don't know. The biggest thing I ever saw blown up was a concrete breakwater."

"You think you can do it?"

Charley shook his head slowly. "I don't know. It's so big, so massive. I don't know enough about blowing up such a structure. If the dynamite isn't put in the right places, it will only blow out, back away from the dam without damaging it. I don't know. All I can do is try."

Charley put the glasses to his eyes and followed the twisting river south. He saw ducks in the quiet pools, saw a deer drinking, watched an osprey dive. "Sure peaceful now," he said, handing the glasses to Donny.

"Won't be for long," Donny said, pointing. Charley's eyes looked out to the horizon, where Donny was pointing. Storm clouds were marshalling forces, building thunderheads.

"Looks bad," Charley said.

"You mean good," Donny corrected him. "A storm will drive those old men who are standing guard to seek shelter. We'll have the place to ourselves. A storm would be just what the doctor ordered."

"But how can we see to set the charges if it is storming?"

"I don't have to see. I know the face of that

dam like I know the palm of my hand. You just tell me where you want the dynamite, and I'll see that it gets there."

"Okay, I'll show you again," Charley said. He scuffed the earth with his boot heels until he had uprooted the sparse tufts of grass from the stingy, sandy soil. With the palm of his hand he smoothed a two-square-foot area of burned-over ground. Then he broke a stick, and using it as a stylus, made a rough sketch of the dam.

"Give me the glasses," he requested, and studied the dam again. He studied the sketch in the sand, then he made four small X's along the apron, examined the structure with the glasses again, and marked four more X's along the face of the dam. Then he marked a place on each abutment. "That should do it." He hesitated, and then added, "I think."

Donny said nothing for several seconds, but then asked, "How are you going to coordinate the fuses so all those charges go off together?"

"Impossible," Charley said. "We're going to run a fuse to only one charge. This one, I think," he said, pointing to a charge beneath the apron. "Then hopefully when it goes off it will trigger all the other charges to explode simultaneously. The blast should do it, trigger the others. If it does, I think the dam will come down."

Donny took the glasses and once more looked at the gleaming white dam. "It sure is big," he said in awed tones. "Maybe we ought to wait. Maybe we ought to think about it, maybe see if we can't find someone with more experience with dynamite to help."

Charley leaned back on an elbow. "It's a little late for that. Don't you think? By this time Betty is probably already in jail, all the people are probably converging on Sayward to light the protest fires. We'd never get there in time to stop them. Anyway, you claim the storm will hide our movements." Charley stopped talking, as though trying to think of some other reason why they should proceed.

Donny smiled. Then he laughed.

"What are you laughing at?" the boy asked.

"All of a sudden you're Gung Ho. All along, it seemed to me that you were the reluctant one. Now all of a sudden you're eager."

Charley smiled too. "Don't you believe I'm eager. Anybody eager for something like this has got to have rocks in his head. Only it seems to me, as long as we have come this far, that it would be a waste not to go through with it. I doubt, if we postponed it now, I could get up enough guts for another try."

A far off rumble of thunder lifted their eyes to the horizon. The black clouds had consolidated and were marching en masse up across the sky. Donny looked at his watch. "In forty-five minutes it will start to get dark. I think we ought to get to the floor of the valley and across the river while we still can see what we're doing."

"Where do we cross?" Charley asked.

"A little way below the first rapids. There's an old, old ford which the people built years ago."

"How deep?"

"Maybe waist deep. Maybe not quite that deep."

They both slipped on their back packs, Donny led the way, scouting the crest. After some minutes, when he found a game trail, they began the descent.

It was easy walking. Obviously many deer used the burn to gorge on buds which the maple shoots had thrust up from the wide waste of fire-scarred stumps. They continued down until they could hear the river. Then they rested, and while they were sitting on a moss-covered log, the marching clouds caught up with the sun and covered it, and the wind came almost all the way around and began to blow briskly out of the west.

The temperature plummeted. "Bet it dropped thirty degrees," Donny said. "Let's get across before dark," Donny said, shifting his pack and getting up.

They walked a little way, broke out of the trees, and following sand bars which marked the shore, moved alongside the rapids. The roar of the water made talk impossible. Donny picked up the pace, and then they were below the rapids and heading out into the stream.

"Be careful," Donny cautioned. "It's very rocky."

The water was much warmer than the air. The current pressed persistently, but never with such force as to make walking dangerous. In the middle of the stream Donny paused and the boy pulled up behind him. They rested briefly, and then continued on across.

Donny turned north when they came to the west shore, and in the last light of day came to the head of the first rapids where the canoe was cached. He found it in seconds, and then as the first wash of rain came slanting down on a gale, the storm broke.

"Hurry," Donny said, lifting the canoe and squeezing beneath it. Charley followed, and huddled in the darkness beneath the boat. Rain drummed on the canvas, and then abruptly the downpour ended, and there was only the whisper of raindrops among the leaves, against the canoe. Then there was no sound of raindrops, and Donny said:

"It's snowing!"

Charley squirmed so he could look out. Inches from his nose white flakes melted as if magically on contact with the still-warm earth.

"How long do we wait?" Charley asked.

"Soon as it snows a little harder we'll move," Donny said.

"You know we've still got to cut a pole. One at least fifteen feet. To tamp the charges in beneath the apron."

"We will. We will. Soon as we get ready to move."

Beneath the canoe the two bodies warmed the trapped pocket of air, and gradually their clothing began to dry. Charley felt sleepy, and it was an effort to keep from closing his eyes.

Now the snow no longer melted on contact with the earth, and Charley could see an edge of whiteness. He closed his eyes and he thought of the girl. He tried to relive last night, recapture the warmth of her caress, the fresh smell of her hair, but he couldn't. He wondered if she was in jail. He wondered too if the protest fires were burning, and was Wilbur already waiting in his truck on the High Road to whisk them to safety?

Donny moved, tilted the canoe back. He got up and Charley stood beside him. Now he felt the snow cold on his cheeks, felt the wind raw in his nostrils.

"We'll drag it," Donny said. "Take hold at the bow." They went slipping and sliding down the muddy trail to the river with the canoe in tow. In an inlet they launched it, and then got out of their packs.

"Now to get a pole," Donny said. He went back in among the trees. Charley followed. In a stand of immature, slender poplars Donny hacked one with his knife until it toppled. Quickly he trimmed it out, and they had a long slender pole to take back to the canoe.

Donny took the stern. Charley knelt in the bow. "We'll stay right tight to the bank out of the main current," Donny said. "You just paddle. I'll take care of the steering."

Then in the wild winging of snow, at the dark edge of the forest where the water ran black, they began to paddle upstream, to blow up the Spirit Flowage dam.

28

In the bow of the canoe Charley leaned forward into the driving snow. He braced his knees to give thrust to his paddle, and he could feel the current try to wrest the blade from his grasp. He wondered if the canoe was moving, wanted to turn, shout to Danny, solicit reassurance that the river's thrust was indeed being overcome. But the roar of water cascading through the flumes was an all-consuming sound.

Suddenly he went over, his face striking the gunwale. He felt the bow of the canoe swerve, felt the current rush to turn it back, felt the craft list, hanging on the edge of disaster. They must have hit a rock. He was paddling frantically to turn the bow, bending the paddle right to the breaking point of the blade. Then the bow came around to reluctantly meet the thrust.

Quickly, within seconds, the roar of water,

the thrust of the current, the lash of wind-driven snow suffocated every sensibility. Like a mountain climber hanging to a tree root above a deep chasm, there was nothing except to persevere, to wield the paddle like a mechanical man, never permitting the coiled-spring strength of his muscles to relax lest he be swept away, perhaps to oblivion.

Gone now the need to talk to Donny. Gone the need to know if they were progressing. Gone the necessity of planting the dynamite charges. Life was submerged and unimportant in this maelstrom of water and wind.

Like an arrow the canoe shot out of the raceway into the calm waters alongside the apron between the flumes. Still Charley paddled frantically, nor did he stop until Donny poked him sharply between the shoulder blades with his paddle. And then he felt at once ashamed that he had permitted himself to be so carried away.

Charley rested his paddle across the gunwales, and expertly Donny ran the canoe alongside the apron and stepped out. While he held the craft broadside to the apron, he motioned for Charley to get out. On the slippery moss-covered concrete apron Charley sank to a sitting position to get his breath, to wait for his heart to subside.

A minute of rest and Donny began dragging the canoe out onto the apron. Charley got up and grasping a gunwale helped. When the craft was out of the water, Donny took Charley's arm. "You okay?" he asked, whispering into Charley's ear. Charley nodded. "Then ready a charge. I'll look for muskrat tunnels."

While Charley knelt and undid a pack, Donny crept along the lip of the apron. Bracing with one hand, he used the other to feel beneath the concrete for places the muskrats might have tunneled.

By the time Charley had a cap wedged down in between a six-stick bundle of dynamite, Donny was probing a muskrat burrow with the long pole. The hole went nearly the length of the pole beneath the apron. He left it there and went back. "I've got a hole," he said, speaking softly into Charley's ear.

Together they moved slowly back to where the stick protruded from beneath the apron. Donny pulled it out. Charley got to his knees, and reaching down, slowly pushed the charge into the burrow. Then with the pole he gently prodded the dynamite bundle as far back as it would go. After the charge was in place, he whispered into Donny's ear, "We have to plug it. With rocks, dirt."

Donny went to the canoe and came back with the trench shovel. Then as he wedged chunks of earth from the river bottom where it came tight up against the concrete, Charley fitted the chunks into the burrow and, with the stick, wedged them tightly up against the charge.

It was slow, exhausting work. A half-hour to set one charge. It would take a long time. Donny found another hole almost dead center of the apron. Charley leaned close to Donny. "This is the one we'll detonate," he said.

He set the cap, got the coiled length of precut fuse from a pack. He wedged the fuse down tight to the cap, taped it firmly in place, and then

191

taped several turns of fuse around the bundle so there would be no chance of it tearing loose.

He put the charge into the hole. Then while Donny gently forced it back to the far end of the burrow, he fed fuse in after it. When it was set and the hole plugged, he uncoiled the rest of the fuse out and across the apron.

By the time they had placed four charges beneath the dam apron, it was midnight and the storm was beginning to abate.

"We have to hurry," Donny said, "the snow will stop falling soon. The cloud cover might go. There'll be at least a piece of moon. We can't take the chance of being discovered."

They had no trouble digging the charges in alongside both abutments. It was only necessary to tunnel down to the concrete, set the charge and fill the hole. Before climbing to the catwalk to place the four charges against the face of the dam, they rested. While they sat on the apron beside the canoe, the snow stopped.

"Let's get going," Donny said.

Charley took the pack with the rope and the last of the four dynamite charges. Donny led the way slowly, pausing often to look and to listen until he was crawling along the crest of the dam. He reached up then, and with a quick catlike movement, swung himself up and onto the catwalk. He reached down, as Charley handed him the dynamite. Then Charley swung himself up, and together they crouched on the iron grillwork of the walk.

They stayed on their knees on the catwalk lest they show a silhouette to any watching eyes.

Charley uncoiled the rope, tied an end to a package of dynamite, set two caps instead of the usual one, and then lowered the charge over the side into the water up against the face of the dam. He let it down twenty feet, and then tied the rope to the catwalk railing.

While he was lowering the charge he kept repeating to himself, "I don't know. I don't know. I only hope. I only hope the water pressure holds them tight enough so they'll blow."

They were lowering the second charge when a guard came out of a stand of trees. They flattened themselves to the catwalk and lay still. The guard came all the way to the steps leading up to the catwalk and then turned and walked back to disappear among the trees.

"They'll be back soon enough," Donny whispered in Charley's ear. "Hurry!"

While Donny cut rope lengths, Charley set fuses. Then each took one of the two remaining charges and hurried to hang them.

"All set?" Donny whispered when the boy was back alongside him.

"All set."

"Well, let's get the hell out of here!"

They went swiftly along the catwalk, dropped to the abutment, and then slid on down onto the apron into the shadows.

"We've got to get the canoe in the water before I light the fuse," Charley said.

Together they dragged the canoe and launched it. Donny got in, put a paddle out to the apron to hold the craft, and then Charley went back

193

to where the fuse stretched like a thin, white snake up across the concrete.

The first match, struck on his silvery belt buckle, broke. The second sputtered and went out. His hands began to tremble. He fought for control. All the hours of tension seemed to come down on him at once. The third match, held between cupped hands, burned brightly. He lowered it and holding the fuse end with one hand put the flame of the match beneath it with the other. The match burned almost all the way back to his thumb and forefinger before, with a wild sputter of brilliance, the fuse began to burn.

For a long moment Charley stood holding the fuse as though hypnotized. "Hurry!" Donny hissed. Charley dropped the fuse, but still he stood as if fascinated by the sputtering fire. "My God, hurry!" Donny hissed again. Still Charley did not move. "Charley!" It was a loud shout. "Charley!" Donny repeated. Charley turned and began walking unsteadily back toward the canoe.

"Get in! My God, get in! They'll see the fuse burning. We'll be trapped. Blown to bits. For God's sake, get in!"

Charley looked back at the fuse. Donny lifted himself in the canoe, and pulled Charley in by a sleeve. Charley slumped, came down slowly, and then half-tumbled, half-stepped into the canoe.

Already there were voices, though they were indistinct. Already there were pounding feet. Then there was a shot, and they heard this, even above the roar of the river.

Donny dug in with the paddle, turned the

canoe, and with a single thrust sent it shooting from the oasis of calm water out into the current. The river hungrily enveloped the craft, lifted it, thrust it skimming forward on the froth of its anger.

Above the cloud curtain parted, and a piece of moon slid into the breach. On the catwalk, oblivious of the explosives beneath them, the two men aimed carbines. But now the men in the canoe could not hear the shots, such was the fury of the maelstrom around them.

Donny shouted, "Paddle, paddle!" But his words were caught up in the spray, suffocated by the sounds of the rapids. But even had he heard, likely Charley would not have heeded.

Right or wrong, Charley knew that at last he had come back to his people, that now he had earned the right to be proud of his ancestry. He had taken up the cause, fought the good fight with every ounce of his strength, his courage. And, he had found love, something he had not dared to hope for after the death of his mother. He felt he was an Indian.

The feeling of exaltation brought him to his feet. He turned, looked back, saw the figures on the catwalk with the little piece of moon behind them. He stood there as if in anticipation, as if waiting to witness the explosion . . .

Then a rock brought the canoe to a shuddering halt. Almost as if in slow motion Charley went over the side. Donny fell forward reaching to save him. Then the white water had Charley, and the canoe swept on by.

Once Donny saw Charley's head briefly and tried to swing the canoe in his direction. Then

Charley disappeared, and Donny stopped paddling and half-raised himself to scan the rapids.

He was in a half-crouch when a shock wave lifted the canoe from the water. He turned in time to see the dam, white in the moonlight, lift perceptibly. He heard a roar. He saw the guards, the catwalk disappear. Then everything disappeared beneath a rushing wall of water.

The floodwaters caught the canoe and almost swamped it. Then like a leaf swirling high in an updraft, the water lifted the craft and bore it down the valley on his foaming crest. Faster and faster, with Donny kneeling and gripping the gunwales, the craft rode high and swift as a flying bird.

Then where the river valley abruptly turned, the flood tossed the canoe aside, thrust it far out into the forest and dropped it along side the High Road. Dazed for a moment, Donny stumbled out of the beached canoe and fell. When he looked up it was to see a wet deer. Its head was hanging and its sides were heaving, a wild wood's creature with eyes wide and luminescent and bewildered in its trembling head.

Below was the roar of the river as the waters of Spirit Flowage bled away. Somewhere down there too was the Sidewalk Indian.

Slowly Donny got to his feet. The deer, head still hanging, haunches trembling, moved slowly away to disappear among the trees. It was over, all over. There was nothing now, nothing more Donny could do.

Epilogue

The vast valley, which once had been covered by the waters of Spirit Flowage, turned green with promise that spring. Then eager families tilled the soil, and when the first yellow flower on a squash vine bloomed, word came south from a Cree village on Canada's Great Bear Lake, that a young man resembling Charley Nightwind had paused there briefly.

Then at harvest time there was another report that someone resembling the Sidewalk Indian was working on a fishing boat off Alaska's shores.

And it is true that they never found the boy's body, though that did not deter them from marking a place for him. So now between the graves of his father and his grandfather in the Burial Grounds on the hill his name is chiseled in a field stone which is shot through with silver flecks of mica.

The stone does not say that he is dead. It only reads:

LOST AT THE DAM SITE

And sometimes an Indian maid comes and stands by the marker in the moonlight, except no one can say what is in her heart, because this is a secret which no one knows about, and about which none would be so cruel as to inquire.

MEL ELLIS

Born and raised in central Wisconsin, a graduate of the University of Notre Dame, Mel Ellis has always been an outdoorsman, fishing and hunting all over America. A former outdoor editor of the *Milwaukee Journal,* he is also the author of several hundred articles published in such well-known magazines as *National Geographic* and *True.* From his knowledge of wildlife and conservation has come the inspiration for many of his works, including: SAD SONG OF THE COYOTE; SOFTLY ROARS THE LION; IRONHEAD; WILD GOOSE, BROTHER GOOSE; RUN, RAINEY, RUN; CARIBOU CROSSING; THE WILD RUNNERS; FLIGHT OF THE WHITE WOLF; PEG LEG PETE; THIS MYSTERIOUS RIVER and NO MAN FOR MURDER. Mr. Ellis presently resides with his wife and family on fifteen acres in Wisconsin.